SPRING TALES

Four Seasons Series
Book Four

SPRING TALES

a short story collection

Four Seasons Series
Book Four

by

Bruce K Beck

AUDACITY BOOKS
WE DARE TO TELL THE TRUTH
New York

This is a work of fiction. Names, characters, businesses, places, events, and incidents are either the products of the author's imagination or used in a fictitious manner.

ISBN 978-1-952031-26-7

This is a first edition from Audacity Books.
Please visit us on the web at www.audacitybooks.com.
For information about rights or purchases,
please email us at info@audacitybooks.com.

Contents

Foreword

Welcome to SPRING TALES, Book Four of Bruce K Beck's **Four Seasons Series** of short story collections.   Readers get to revisit the seven sets of handsome couples we first met in summer and grew to love even more deeply in autumn and winter. Seven sets of narrators and the people who love them as they strive to build better lives and stronger relationships during the magical season of rebirth and renewal.

As before, New York City provides the perfect backdrop for our stories. Hearts blossom just as surely as the flowering trees and springtime gardens do. Welcome to stronger families, tough decisions, deepening needs, chances to finally get things right, and perhaps a wedding or two!

New York City, May 15, 2024

This book is dedicated to those, like me,
who love New York City in all seasons.

It was a Sunday morning in April. It might have been unremarkable, except that I was keenly aware of how much I loved spending quiet time with Tommy. And that was partly because it was a year —nearly to the day—since he had phoned and asked me to let him come to New York and stay with me. Nearly a year since our reunion. Half a lifetime since we had last been close, just after high school graduation.

I was scrambling eggs—one of the few kitchen tasks I had bothered with since Tommy came to live with me. He was so much better at cooking than I had ever been. And he seemed to love it—cooking, and living with me. I had a silly grin on my face, I'm sure, as I watched him carefully making coffee with our new vacuum pot. I had never had the patience to weigh and grind the beans for my morning brew.

Tommy seemed to have patience for many precise tasks. He's a lawyer, after all. So whether he was reading a legal text or sautéing chicken breasts for our dinner or tending to the care and feeding of my heart, Tommy was always focused and thorough. I shouldn't have been so shocked by what followed. But I was.

As we sat down to our Sunday breakfast, Tommy said, "Bri, why don't we get married?" I didn't do anything gross, like snorting Tommy's excellent coffee—now generously laced with hot milk—or choking on a warm buttered croissant, but I did feel … jolted, I suppose. The question seemed to come from nowhere.

It wasn't that I had never dreamed of legalizing our union. I had yearned for it for decades, really. It was just that the fairy-tale quality of the last year had left me grateful for what I had and less than eager to tempt fate. True, Tommy's divorce from Nancy would be final in a week or so. True, we could go to the City Clerk any fine day after that to purchase a marriage license.

"It's easier than ever," Tommy said. "Since the COVID lockdown, there are online steps available. You won't even need to take a day off from work, Bri." I smiled and feigned interest in my breakfast. And I didn't have a ready reply. "I think it's wise for us to do this soon," Tommy continued. "The haters want to overturn Obergefell, and they may very well do it. But if we're married, no one can undo that."

Sound legal advice, surely. "Are you certain this is what you want?" I asked Tommy. I instantly felt like an idiot, but the question was still hanging in the air. And the peace and harmony of our quiet Sunday morning suddenly vaporized as surely as if an April storm cloud had decided to enter our apartment.

"Talk to me, Bri Baby," he said. "Your happiness is all I want." I got up from the table and walked behind him, putting my arms around Tommy's glorious shoulders. I leaned in and rested my head against his, ear to ear.

"I gave you my heart when I was five, Tom Cat," I said. "And I gave you my body—or what's left of it—last year. You own everything that's mine to give. Maybe I'm wondering if that might be enough. Or maybe I'm just scared."

"Tommy wrapped his arms around mine and said, "Sorry, Bri. I didn't mean to frighten you. I thought you'd want it as much as I do."

"I do," I said. "See, I'm already getting into the spirit of things! It's just that you have family to consider, and would it be creepy to go out and get a marriage license the day after your divorce decree is final? And do we need to rush into this? And what if it changes our relationship? I'm so fucking happy with our lives just the way they are. I don't need change, Tommy. I just need you."

Most of it sounded lame to me, but at least I got my thoughts out into the open. "Come here, Brian," he said as he pushed away from the dining table. I'm still trim enough that I could sit on Tommy's lap without inflicting damage. He cradled me in his arms and began to rock me ever so slightly. It conjured up images of a childhood I never experienced.

"Bri, you took care of me when we were kids."

"Isn't that a little dramatic?" I asked.

"No, it's honest," Tommy said. "You were there, Brian. You talked to me and dried my tears after Dad humiliated me. You rubbed salve on my welts after he beat the shit out of me, and you helped me into my pajamas so I could get some sleep. You were my witness. If you hadn't been there, I might not trust my memories. You comforted me, Bri."

"Well, maybe we comforted each other," I suggested.

"Let's not quibble about who did what to whom. I'm just saying that I owe you my life, Bri, and now that we're together, I want to care for you. I want to protect you. I want to give you all the security there is in this crazy world. And if we're married, I can do a better job of it."

As legal arguments go, Tommy's had everything in its favor. And as emotional arguments go, it was even more persuasive. I had no choice but to drop my armor. Mostly. "Of course you're right, Tommy," I said. "I want marriage as much as you do. But I can't quite wrap my brain around it today. Could we table the topic? Maybe come back to it next weekend?"

"Of course, Bri," he said. "Whenever you want." I felt like a jerk for skirting such an important issue, but I felt relieved to be avoiding such a big decision. For a while, anyway. Tommy avoided the subject all afternoon, as I knew he would. The ball was in my court. And it was up to me to make the next serve.

"I'm sorry," I said to Tommy at about 5:00 while he was in the kitchen starting dinner. He was standing at the stove sautéing onions as I walked up behind him and wrapped myself around his beautiful torso. Tommy in my arms always threatened me with sensory overload. The added scent of onions cooking in olive oil had me in a swoon state.

"Sorry for what, Bri?" he asked.

"For being such a jerk this morning."

"Oh, were you jerky this morning, Bri?" he asked. "Talk to me."

"Yes, well, you were too polite to notice, I think. I suppose I'll have to expect that—if I intend to marry a Southern gentleman." Tommy wheeled on me with a look of pure joy on his face.

"Brian Henry Ledbetter, don't fuck with me!" he said. "This veneer of Southern civility is way thin, as you well know." I grabbed Tommy with all my strength and planted a deep kiss on his sweet mouth.

"You're all I've ever wanted, Tommy," I said once I had come up for air. "You know that. And you know you'll have to be patient with me." Tommy turned off the gas, took my hand, and led me toward the bedroom. "What about dinner?" I asked.

"Fuck dinner," he said.

"No, fuck *me!*" I suggested. And that's what he did.

I told Jenna about "the proposal," of course. I told her nearly everything. We shared lunch on Monday, as usual. She and Tommy adored each other— to my great relief—so I didn't have to explain much about the situation. The three of us were family. Jenna seemed to understand that I had been caught off guard.

"You can't play games with marriage," Jenna said to me. "You have to be all in. You can't just decide it's a good idea from a legal standpoint. You have to take vows, Brian, and you have to want that union with every sinew in your heart. Otherwise, it's a disaster. I never told you. It was a long time ago. Or so it seems." My, my, can't friends be full of surprises! Jenna took a deep breath or two and continued:

"I was twenty-one. A senior at Yale. Daniel is a nice guy. Smart. Handsome. My parents in Skokie know his parents in Skokie. Everyone wanted the marriage. I won't say it was arranged. I wasn't absent while all those plans were being made. But it unfolded at a point in my life when I sometimes let things happen to me. And then I woke up the next morning in bed with a man I didn't love.

"Now, I know you love Tommy with your whole heart, and I know he worships you. So, love is not the issue here. But Brian, if marriage is not your dream, then forget it. What you have now is perfect as it is. But if marriage is what you want, then I'll proudly be your flower girl, or your maid ... matron of honor, or your best friend, or whatever you want me to be. I'll give you away: I'll tell the preacher and the whole congregation that you will make the best fucking spouse on the planet. Because I believe that with all my heart."

God bless Jenna! She's not one to mince words. "Thanks, sweetie," I said. "I'm dealing pretty well with the whole thing, except for Tommy's family. I just don't know if it's worth stirring up a lot of drama."

"It's not up to them, is it?" she said. A good point. Jenna had met both of Tommy's children, of course—Brian back in the fall and Melissa in the winter. I knew that she and Brian got along very well indeed. But I still shudder when I remember Jenna's dinner party, when Melissa pretty much called her a fag hag and an old maid—if not in so many words.

"I think Brian will be fine with the whole thing," Jenna said.

"I agree."

"And I think Melissa will come around in record time. She quite likes you, Bri. In case you didn't notice."

"Maybe," I said. "But I have no illusions about how much happier Melissa would be if she had her daddy all to herself."

"It's a girl thing, Brian," Jenna said. "You can't fight it."

"No, I don't think I'd want to try. But what worries me most is Nancy." There! I said it out loud. I hadn't wanted to go there, even in my own mind. And I certainly hadn't mentioned Tommy's soon-to-be ex-wife to him. But I believed we owed her something. Some ... consideration? I didn't know what it was, but I felt a deep need to get it right.

Jenna looked at me with a pitying glance and a head shake, and she said, "Right out of the age of chivalry, that boy!" I knew it was a line from a '40s movie. I could hear Lee Patrick saying it, but I couldn't remember which picture. As if it mattered. "Look, Brian," Jenna said, "I'm not going to tell you that you won and Nancy lost. It's not that simple. But it doesn't have to be complicated, either."

I wasn't so sure. Winning and losing both fill me with dread. Maybe that's why I can't bring myself to play Monopoly. I hate being a loser, but if my victory means someone else's defeat, then I want no part of it. "I don't know the woman," Jenna said, "but I do know a small group of other people who love Tommy. So I'm guessing she's got some quality and spine to her. Am I right?"

"Indeed."

"Then invite her to the wedding. You two were school friends, right? Invite her, Brian. *Don't* make Tommy do it. *Don't* send an invitation in the mail. Just get on the phone and tell her that you and Tommy are getting married, and you both want her to be there. Don't wait until the kids have a chance to tell her. Don't let her be the last to know. Tell her first. She'll respect you for that—more than you know. I'm guessing that she'll show up. In fact, I'm laying odds in favor of it."

My, my. A lot to think about. I rather floated through the rest of the week. Workdays, dinners with Tommy—mostly his own creations—and, of course, perfect nights with Tommy holding me and keeping me safe. Quiet mornings when I felt so happy that I could easily have made it out the door even without a cup of Tommy's brilliant coffee to stimulate me. But I was only buying time. I would have to face the music on the weekend. Fortunately, I always liked the Wedding March.

"How do you think we should handle this?" I asked Tommy on Saturday morning. "The wedding, I mean. Will the kids be free in June, do you think?"

Tommy flashed me his wonderful smile. "Are you sure it's what you want, Bri?"

"Certain," I answered with near-total honesty. "A weekend in early June, maybe? Before Pride gets into full swing. And *not* close to Father's Day, please. Of course, we could also elope," I suggested. "I've always wanted to go to Niagara Falls."

"Then I'll take you there—right after the ceremony!" It was time for a serious kiss, to seal the deal. Tommy's kiss had always made my heart flutter, starting with the first time we "accidentally" brushed lips, when we were seven or so. The mere notion of sharing kisses with Tommy every day for the rest of my life filled me with such sweetness that I wondered where the wedding trepidations had come from.

"Jenna told me about a guy who performs weddings. His name is Jim, I think, and he's ordained by some church or other. Father Jim officiates at a lot of gay unions, so he knows how to make everyone comfortable and how to file the right papers."

"I'll get on it first thing Monday morning," Tommy said.

And then it seemed time to usher the elephant out of the room. I looked Tommy squarely in the eyes and said, "As soon as we set a date, I'll call Nancy, to invite her." Tommy grabbed me and held me close.

"If I loved you any more, my heart would burst," he said. That was a feeling I understood well.

"Tommy, I just want to get this right," I said. "If we start our new life together on the back of someone else's pain, then ..."

"Hush, Bri Baby," he said. "We're all about joy. There's no room for pain here." If I were the praying sort—and I am not—I would have echoed Tommy's declaration. Even so, I found myself thinking, *Amen.* I may have actually murmured it. Maybe.

And that's how we began to plan our wedding. Not that it seemed a done deal. So many odds and ends not yet connected. Would the kids be free? Would the kids even want to witness their "old man" wedding this home-wrecker? But we pushed on and chose a date: The first Sunday in June. And then it was up to me to spring into action.

"Brian, I'm not shocked to hear your news," Nancy said when I phoned her on Monday. "I was expecting it, I suppose. Still, it might take me a moment to process the whole concept."

"Take all the time you need."

Bruce K Beck

"May I ask why *you* are inviting me to the wedding, Brian?"

"Of course," I said. "That's easy. You're family, Nancy. I want you to be with us."

"And Tom?"

"He wants you to be happy."

"Yes, well, I promised MaryEllen McGinley—you remember her, Brian: She was MaryEllen Lashley when we were growing up."

"Of course I remember her. She had the reddest hair in Baltimore County."

"Yes, well, she still does—with a little help from Clairol. But who's talking? Anyway, MaryEllen took a house at the shore for the summer, and she asked me to join her the first week in June. I said I would. I can probably change it. She'll be there all summer. Will you give me a little time to sort this out?"

"Of course," I said. "Take all the time you need. Nancy, we'd love you to be with us if it's comfortable for you. But there's no pressure. God knows we've all lived with plenty of that." And then I decided I had better shut up and let the process work in its own way.

"Thanks, Brian. I'll get back to you in a few days."

"So, Bri, is it true—that Dad is going to make an honest man of you?" Brian asked. He phoned me— after texting to schedule a time, of course—and I was delighted to hear from him.

"What do you think?" I asked.

"I think you make him very happy, and I think that's all that matters."

"But how do *you* feel, Brian?" I asked. "I'd like to know."

"Well, the truth is, I liked Mom and Dad together. Apparently, I liked it more than they did. I'm learning how many things around me are none of my business. This is obviously one of them."

"Not really," I said. "Your Dad and I both want to keep you close. Your happiness is important to us, and to the lives we're building together."

"So what if I say, 'No, I think your marriage is a bad idea.' Will you cancel?"

"Fat chance," I said. "We haven't waited half our lives to be together to let some brat come between us."

"It's a good thing I love you," Brian said.

"Yes, well, just don't get me started on how I sometimes yearn to think of you as the son I never had. That's much too painful to share." It was true, of course.

"Will I have to call you Bri Daddy?"

"You can call me anything you like. Except Fuck Face. I don't answer to that."

"I'll work on it."

One child down and one to go.

♏

"Which one of you will be the bride?" Melissa asked when she called me.

"Don't be a smart-ass," I suggested. "It doesn't suit you. And you're not smart enough to tangle with me, in case you didn't notice."

"I did, actually," she said. "I know when I'm out-bitched."

"Yes, well, I told your dad I have doubts about how you might behave on our special day, and he assured me you would be civil and supportive. Does that sound likely to you?"

"Well, it certainly sounds like Dad. He has always expected the best of us. And sometimes he's actually gotten it."

"How about this June?" I asked. "What's the forecast?"

"Warm and sunny, last I heard."

"Good," I said. "Did you invite your friend Emma to the wedding?"

"I did," Melissa said. "She wants to be there, but she's not certain she'll be finished with all her course work in time to leave Georgetown that early in June. I hope she can make it. I know you like her very much. I know you like her better than you like me."

"Emma is a charming young woman. You, my dear, are family. It's different." I nearly quoted Fay Bainter in *JEZEBEL*, something like, "As Pres's wife, [read: Tom's daughter] you are naturally welcome here at Halcyon. But you, my dear, are welcome for yourself." But I couldn't quite see the point in a '30's movie reference when no one seems to know anything about the past, anyway. Oh, well.

"Jenna is looking forward to seeing you again," I said.

"I'll bet."

"Really. She said you remind her of herself. I don't see it, but she does," I said.

"I wish," she said. "Tell her that gives me big shoes to fill. No, don't tell her that! Just tell her I'm looking forward to seeing her again, too. And tell her I may have developed a hint of humanity since I saw her last."

"Will do," I said.

I can't tell you why it took me so long to figure it out. It was so obvious: All we needed to do was schedule the wedding for the shore. There is a hotel, after all, not far from the beach house. Surely they would have an event space. And we could book a room for Jenna. And anyone else we needed to put up. Nancy could keep her plans with MaryEllen and just come to the ceremony—if she so chose. Hell, she could bring MaryEllen with her!

Brian and Melissa both would be close enough to Baltimore and/or their colleges to just come for the day and get swiftly back to their lives. And maybe their friends might consider coming, too. I had good feelings about inviting Brian's friend Jeremy, and, of course, Melissa's friend Emma. Yes, it all seemed suddenly possible.

The best part, of course, was all the alone time Tommy and I could share at the beach house—after the ceremony. "It's perfect, Bri," Tommy said when I shared my ideas. "Like you!" And once we had committed to a venue for the ceremony, I started to feel at ease about the whole thing for the first time. Until I remembered Father Jim.

"I like the Delaware shore," he said when I phoned him about our marriage plans, "and I have an extra day or two for travel that week. Yes, my ordination papers qualify me to officiate in Delaware. No problem. Just be sure to order the marriage license online no more than 30 days before the ceremony. And, if I'm not mistaken, you and Tom will have to appear together at the County Clerk's office, or whatever it's called, ID in hand, at least twenty-four hours before the ceremony, to collect the certificate. Don't forget the divorce papers. Tom will know how to handle all of that." Of course he would.

"Thanks, Rev," I said.

"You can call me Father."

"Not Daddy?"

"Too personal."

"Okay, Father," I said. "I've never had a father I actually liked, but I think I can adjust to the concept."

"Bless you, my son."

It was a real New York springtime: shockingly verdant and yet frequently cool. Each wave of new blossoms filled the air—and my heart—with joy and seduction. Tommy and I took some weekend strolls through Central Park, of course. How could we not? How could we avoid joining all the other young lovers who lose their worries and fears to the promise of renewal and rebirth?

It was always a treat to be out in the world with Tommy. Everything I really needed I could savor from the confines of my apartment—*our* apartment. But the richness of the cityscape made it all better. Everything seemed to be falling into place—the wedding plans, of course, but also Tommy had filed for, and been granted, reciprocal bar membership. Maryland and New York are not on those terms, as it happens, but DC does have that arrangement. And

Tommy's a bar member there. So, New York accepted him.

And that's why, in mid-May, he told me, "Bri, I got a great offer from a fine, old law firm. I think I should take it. Come September, you could be living with Salary Man," Tommy told me.

"As long as it's what he wants," I said. "I think it's about for better or for worse, for richer or for poorer—enough of that! Do what makes you happy, Tom Cat."

"That's my plan, Bri!"

"Damn!" I had a sudden thought. "What are we going to wear to the wedding? I don't think Ts and trunks will cut it."

"Seersucker suits," Tommy suggested.

"You're joking," I said. "Do they still make those? I haven't seen seersucker since I was a little kid in short pants."

"I think they do still make them," Tommy said. "I'll do some homework. What color?"

"Blue is nice," I said.

"Yes, but maybe a bit ordinary."

"Not green, I think," I said. "It doesn't feel right for a wedding, somehow. And not yellow, either. We'll be long past daffodils come June. What about pink?"

"Possibly," Tommy said. "Pink has nearly everything going for it. But I think lavender would be ideal. Yes, lavender. There must be a stuffy old clothing company somewhere in the Northeast that makes things like that. Or we'll go to a tailor."

"So, I'm going to tie the knot with Thomas Robert Whitaker, Esq., while we're both wearing lavender seersucker suits?" I asked. "Perfect!"

"So long as Brian Henry Ledbetter agrees to be mine, I'll take him in a burlap bag, a frayed jock-strap, or nothing at all."

"We're really going to do this, aren't we?" I said.

"Looks like it. There's still time to back out, you know."

"Not on your life! When will I ever get another chance to wear a lavender seersucker suit?"

It was the most glorious New York springtime I could remember. Cool but verdant. The leaf buds on the trees began to form quite early. Then the crocuses; then the daffodils. And then the cherry blossoms, so lush you could nearly hear them pop. Noah had never been to the Brooklyn Botanic Gardens in cherry blossom season, so I took him, naturally.

It was a challenge. *We* had been nearly as busy as Mother Nature that season. So, for a rare Sunday off, all I really wanted was to spend the day in bed with my perfect mate. Just the two of us. But an angel of my better nature put a smile on my face as I said, over breakfast, "Let's go to Brooklyn!"

"Toby, this is amazing," Noah said. "I knew about the Brooklyn Museum when I was a kid in Connecticut. Because of the Egyptian collection. And I finally got there a few years ago for the Frida Kahlo show. But I had no idea there were gardens next door."

"Stick with me," I said. "The best is yet to be."

"I intend to," Noah said, as he tightened his grip on my arm. I believed him, of course. I had to believe that Noah wanted to stay with me and grow old with me and share every moment of our lives. With me.

We were still young, of course. I wasn't yet forty. Noah even younger. But I had seen terrible things happen to people. Terrible pain and degradation. Even death. But I think loneliness is worst of all.

That spring Noah glowed with vitality—that Sunday and every day. I had told him recently that when I photographed him, I never had to worry about his lighting because he always carried his own key light! So, you can tell me that's lofty metaphor coming from a lowly still photographer, but I meant it. My Noah seemed lit from within. And I fancied that somehow his radiance illuminated the darkest places in my soul.

The wisteria—always my favorite—had just started to give us a preview of how its lazy glory would festoon all the pergolas in the gardens—in about two weeks. I reached for the nape of Noah's perfect neck. His boyish auburn curls against the whiteness of his skin had always fascinated me. Nearly as much as the taste of him. I restrained myself. We walked on.

And then I asked, "Noah, when you went to bed with me for the first time, last July, did you think I'd be your chocolate Easter bunny this spring?"

"I didn't just think it, I knew it," he answered without hesitation. "Why do you ask, Toby?"

"Why does anybody who's desperately in love ask stupid questions?" Noah paused us on the path, on a little ridge, overlooking the Japanese garden, and he kissed me so sweetly that, well, as we used to say in the South, I didn't know whether to shit or go blind. Fortunately, I did neither.

"Let's get something to eat," I suggested. And that's what we did. When we got home to the loft, both of us were more than ready for some bed time.

I had been walking around with at least half an erection all afternoon, and I sensed—and saw—that Noah was in very much the same fix. The beauty of his body, the creaminess of his skin, and the warmth of his scent all conspired to make me tingle like a schoolboy who's about to get his first hand job.

"On your back, young man," I whispered.

"Yes, Sir!" And with the grace and flexibility Noah had maintained since his days as a dancer, he assumed the position—legs over his head; arms forward welcoming me to his world. And it was the only world I cared to inhabit. Noah's welcome made me want not just to please him: *That* I had probably done reasonably well for nearly a year.

I had never really doubted my ability to give Noah pleasure. Or even satisfaction, maybe. But that quiet Sunday evening in April, I felt ... challenged, I suppose. It didn't seem enough to be a considerate lover. I yearned to be a better man. I think that was it. It didn't matter that Noah clung to me with the purest need to have me deep inside him; to blend my body and my soul with his; to become as one complete being where there had been two. It didn't matter that our lovemaking was as explosive as it had ever been. Perhaps even more so.

"Toby, I never thought I could feel the way you make me feel," Noah said when we had come down from our high. I answered him with a renewed embrace of his perfect body. I had no words. Neither of us had much to say for the rest of the evening. Our smiles did most of the talking.

We could have pulled the shades over the skylights as we prepared for sleep. But Noah loves moonlight nearly as much as I do. Even the brightest supermoon leaves me feeling blessed by the silvery calm it projects. We left the skylights uncurtained, as we often did. And we settled into our plush nest of goose down and fine, high-thread-count cotton.

Just as we had done most nights since July, Noah let me hold him and press my body to his. There was something about my crotch against the perfection of Noah's ass that always made me feel safe. Something about his strength, I think. The powerful dynamo in my arms wanted to surrender to me. It was barely even sexual, although I knew I would cycle erections all through the night, as men do.

As always, I knew I was home when I could press my face against the nape of Noah's neck and drink in his scent. When his breathing settled into a soft, near-snore, I expected to lose consciousness, as usual. But Noah in my arms, in the moonlight that night, made me start to weep. I had no explanation for my tears.

It didn't seem to come from sadness, for surely I was experiencing none. Nobody had left anybody. Nobody was helping anybody in or out of bed or wiping anybody's ass. Nobody was disposing of anybody's ashes or dealing with wills or codicils. Nobody was desperate for work or money or food. Not in our household, anyway. But I couldn't lose the feeling of unease that had begun to chill my soul.

The next morning, we were back in the grind. Perry was due to arrive at nine with Gabriela Simón in tow. She wanted to spy on a fall-into-winter fashion shoot, and I was always happy to let her get an early peek at what I was doing. Designers were happy, too, of course. Gabriela had a certain make-or-break influence on other fashion influencers.

Elijah arrived bright and early, as always. And, as always, he was as sunny as Sol himself. But I detected an extra note of cheerfulness that made me wonder. Noah was in the shower, so it was just the two of us in the kitchen as Elijah made coffee and readied his makeup things.

"What's going on?" I asked.

Elly looked a bit startled, as if he imagined his new radiance was invisible. But he considered my question and then answered: "Perry asked me to marry him. What do you think, Boss?"

"I think you two are both exceptionally lucky. Unless you intend to leave me, Elly. In that case, it's the worst idea ever."

"Nobody's leaving nobody," he said.

"Good. You know I couldn't run my business without you, Elly." It was true, really. Elijah took care of all the nagging details, freeing me to get behind the camera and "make magic." "Come here," I said. Elijah complied. I embraced him and held him close to my heart. "My little brown boy is all grown up now," I said. "You'll make Perry a perfect mate. You'll be the husband he deserves. The husband he once hoped *I* could be. And he'll be the husband that maybe you once thought maybe *I* could be. This is starting to sound sick. And it's all ancient history."

"I get the message, Boss," Elijah said. "And thanks."

"For?"

"For pushing Perry in my direction." I sputtered a bit, but it was true, of course. I was the one who organized an ice-skating party in Bryant Park and then took Noah back to bed so that Elly and Perry could have alone time. I doubt I had ever tried matchmaking, but I certainly scored with beginner's luck.

I was a little nervous that morning. It wasn't about the fashions or the preparations for the shoot. I had seen everything as it loaded in. I knew we were ready to go. I knew Perry would send me great models. I knew Gabby was a big fan of James Ferrucci's work. As well she might be. His fabrics were always like something you'd want to have for dessert. And the way he cut them: his clothes draped the human frame with such lascivious devotion that there was an anatomy lesson in every rag. Those FIT babies certainly learn how to work the shit out of a bolt of cloth.

Jimmy arrived a few minutes later and began to enjoy a cup of Elly's excellent coffee. The calm before the storm. Jimmy sat at the same counter where he used to blow me after a photo shoot—maybe thinking that it would help me to make him look more important. Probably just because he wanted to blow me. I never refused him. He's a nice man. I'll take a blow job any day from a nice man rather than a "hot" man. But that was then. When Noah entered my life, everything changed.

Jimmy had the usual preshow jitters. I assured him his work was perfect, as always. I assured him I would deliver all the images he needed to sell the new line. And I assured him that Gabby would love every piece in the new collection, especially the garment he chose to "leak" a photo of.

I was calm about the shoot, but I was nervous because we hadn't seen Gabriela in a few months. True, she thanked us warmly for the "exclusive" photos Noah and I sent her in January. Our photo shoot—between Christmas and New Year's—had been so joyous and free that we were happy to share the results with someone who could do some good for our careers.

I "leaked" some of the more explicit photos to Gabriela with the strict understanding that they were private and off the record. Noah and I both knew there was always a chance that these "private" photos might be "leaked" in turn. So we both decided which images we felt showed us off at our very best. And which ones would do us the least harm. Just in case they went public.

It wasn't really nerves I was experiencing. It was more like an awareness that every shoot has the potential to boost or sink. It was different for Noah. Noah is beautiful. Noah will always be beautiful. I knew he could easily get quality work for the next three decades, anyway. Probably longer. Provided he never gets fat, of course. My career is different. People like Gabriela Simón get to decide if I am relevant. My photographic style—whatever that means—could easily become passé overnight. I hope I can be forgiven a jitter or two.

The models arrived. They were perfect for the clothes, of course. Perry knows his shit. The natural light that streamed through my skylights was perfectly filtered and reflected. My lighting instruments behaved. They don't always, but they did that Monday. And the great galvanized octopus on the ceiling purred along, delivering its quiet blessing of filtered air. No sweat and no goose bumps. Always my goal—unless of course it's a swimsuit shoot, in which case I've been known to hike up the heat in search of a glow that cool and comfy bodies never display.

Things went so well that we wrapped a little early. Jimmy kissed up to Gabriela, of course. He also kissed up to me. Even though it was unnecessary. In the old days, Jimmy would have waited until everyone else had left and then demonstrated his gratitude orally. It had been fun. Did I miss it? Maybe a little. And then Jimmy was off—to his studio, no doubt, to make notes on last-minute corrections to the line. The star dress was evident. And the dress Jimmy could "give" Gabby was mostly decided. But there was always more to do.

"Perry," I said to my business partner and former lover, "thanks for doing everything right, as always. Do models keep getting better looking, or is it my imagination?"

"Hybrid vigor," he said. "The new crop is breathtaking. And we're less obligated to assign them to racial stereotypes. Jimmy doesn't have to design for White or Black or Brown or Yellow people. He just designs for people. And his clothes look great. That sweater set thing that Noah modeled? How amazing was that?"

"I was afraid I might cream in my pants while we were shooting that," I said.

"You weren't the only one," Perry said.

"Per," I said quietly, "a little bird had some news for me this morning. A little prophet, actually. A *mighty* prophet, I should add. And not one to be trifled with."

"Toby, I adore Elijah. I guess I've known that for a few years. But it never seemed likely that he could have feelings for me. I would never have gone there if you hadn't pushed us together. I'm grateful for that push."

"Just remember, Old Friend, if you hurt my Elly, I'll track you down, cut off your very pretty balls, and eat them for breakfast. And I can see your perfect cock wrapped in soft black leather hanging from the light fixture in the kitchen. Do I make myself clear?"

"Crystal."

"So, we understand each other. Good." I was satisfied—as much as is possible—that the two of them were on the right track. They were, after all, the only two people on Earth, besides Noah, for whom I had deep feelings. Maybe.

Gabriela took me aside just then, just before Perry would sweep her off to a very glamorous dinner, no doubt. She said, "Toby, why haven't you married that boy? Do you think there's perfection waiting around every corner?"

"Gabby, I don't know what to say."

"Most people say, 'Will you marry me?' or so I'm told. Look, Toby, I've seen a lot of talent in my time, and I don't give a fuck what happens to most of them. But I can spot a match made in Heaven, even from my evil perch here at the Gates of Fashion Hell. I'm willing to do everything I can do for you and Noah. I would help out even if one of you were 'uglier than homemade sin,' as people said where I grew up. Never mind where. Or when. Fortunately, that is not the case. Let me help you."

"But Gabby, it's not just up to me."

"Yeah, like Noah is going to say, 'No, Tobias, I will not marry you.' When that happens, you come to me, Toby. I have rings that will fit on any of your appendages. Meanwhile, I never thought I would have to tell you to grow some balls. I've seen yours, as you well know. I thought they were more than adequate. Apparently, I was wrong."

"Isn't that hitting below the belt?" I asked.

"No, it's just a reminder that you should always punch above your weight. Do I have to go and tell Noah that *he* should propose to *you*? I will, Toby. You know that, don't you? Noah looks so handsome, just at this moment, standing there talking to Perry and Elijah. I think I'll just get the whole fucking family involved."

"Thanks for your interest, Darling," I said. "But I think I can handle this."

"See that you do." And then she called out, "Perry! Take me to dinner!" And that's what he did. Of course.

"What was Gabby so intense about?" Noah asked me when we were alone.

"She thinks we should get married."

"What do you think?"

"I think it's a great idea."

"But?"

"But maybe I think we could have figured that out on our own," I said. "And maybe there's something I need to do first. Noah, I don't know quite how to explain this."

"So, don't explain it," Noah said. "Just tell me what you feel."

"Yes, well, I feel richly blessed. I guess."

"And? Look, Tobicito, I can't help if you won't tell me what you feel. As long as you don't feel the need to shoot someone on Fifth Avenue, I think we can deal with it. Besides, that obsession is already taken."

"I want to do good," I said. "There, I've said it out loud. I want to do good in the world. That's all I know."

"Darling, did you think I would be shocked?"

"I didn't know what to think. You've made me so completely happy, Noah, and maybe because of that I just need to ... do something ... more. I won't go all evangelical on you. I don't have a single Southern Black preacher in my DNA, as far as I know. And I've never been on the road to Damascus. Aleppo, once, but never mind. Noah, I need a calling. I just don't know what it is."

"I'm glad you shared that, Toby. It explains a lot of what I've been sensing lately. Things I didn't have words for."

"It has nothing to do with my love for you, Noah," I said.

"I think you're quite wrong, Toby," he said. "I think that once we love, it becomes boundless. I feel it, too. I just didn't know I needed to do something about it."

"Noah, I need you so desperately. I can't even figure out how to ..."

"Hush, Toby. You're the strongest man I know. And the best man I know. And don't get me started on how sexy you are, because that's off topic. Could I make a suggestion?"

"Of course."

"You want to make a difference, Toby?"

"Yes."

"Queer kids," Noah said.

"What?"

"Do something. I'll try to help you. Look, I had a fairly easy time of it, but I had a neighbor who took a leap and was found dangling from a rope tied to a Colonial hayloft. When we were fourteen. And that was when social media nastiness was still in its infancy. And another classmate of mine came home from his first year at Harvard and blew his brains out in a ditch by the county road. Kids need help, Toby. I know you had a rough time of it, and I wish I could have been there to comfort the beautiful little boy you were. But you and I are survivors, Toby. Our brains are wired for survival. Not all kids have that luxury."

"But what can I do?" I asked. "I'm a photographer. How could I make a difference in a queer kid's life?"

"The man I love can do anything," Noah said. "I've seen it. I've felt him reach inside me and fix things that were wrong."

"I know there are outreach programs for gay kids—for lots of troubled kids. But they seem inadequate to me. Since you brought it up, Beauty."

"Uh, huh."

"'It gets better' is true, of course, but that's not enough to save kids who are ready to die."

"Nope."

"Will you really help me, Noah? Do you really think we can make a difference?"

"I think we can do anything we decide to do. You'll know what it looks like, Toby. And I'll help you any way I can. It might take a lot of overnights, however. Luckily, we have the right bed for the job."

"Not to mention the moonlight," I added. "You're not just fucking with me?" I asked.

"Not just."

"In that case, when we've sorted this all out, will you do me the honor of becoming my husband?"

"Can't we just elope?" I asked Charley in early April. It seemed an eternity since we had first decided on marriage, and yet surely the details had only been bouncing around for a month or so.

"We can do anything my perfect Petey wants," he said.

"I wish I knew what I want—besides you, Darling." That earned me a deep kiss. It helped. The last month had been both blissful and stressful. I had nothing to be agitated about, really. Charley had asked me to marry him. I had accepted his proposal. The rings were ordered, and Cartier not only sized them for us, but they also engraved them. The wide gold band I would give Charley on our wedding day read, inside, "Please be mine forever." And the matching band that Charley would give me read, "My perfect happiness."

Surely Charley and I were ideally matched—if indeed that is a possibility for two imperfect creatures. Or, rather, the imperfect creature that I was paired with Charley's godlike perfection. His beauty astounded me at every turn, I must say. The smile that greeted me every morning; the sparkle in Charley's eyes when he told me he loved me; the warmth of his scent any time of day or night; the sweetness of his kiss; the perfect roundness of his buttcheeks, which always make me want to hold them; the glory of his majestic cock with its regal honor guard.

And speaking of the guards who honor His Majesty's majesty, I have to say Charley has the most exquisite balls I've ever encountered. And I've encountered more than I should probably admit. The size and shape and weight of Charley's pair is impressive, true, but it's the way they express his feelings that dazzles me. They dance to the music of the moment. They never hide from me. They never deny my touch or my taste.

But Charley's perfect orbs are not mine to own. I'm still trying to learn to accept that reality. I hope I *do* own a part of Charley's heart. A substantial part. He said the whole thing is mine. I'd settle for half. Or three-quarters, maybe. A man has obligations, after all. "Give me three-quarters of your heart and I'll let you keep the rest for family and friends." That seemed a reasonable demand.

I'm not certain I was doing anything very reasonable that spring. It was about wedding plans, mostly. There were so many options! The City Clerk's Office, of course. Sometimes I thought that might be our best choice. But then, Ajmal had offered us the comfort of his midtown penthouse—for the ceremony and for our honeymoon.

We're talking about the Ajmal who is the hottest man—besides Charley—I have ever known. And the same Ajmal who fucked me silly the previous fall while Charley was away on business in Singapore— leaving me alone all those lonely months. True, it only happened the one time. But I wasn't the one to follow up with, "I can't do this again because my heart belongs to Charley." It was more like Ajmal saying, "I can't do this again because your heart belongs to Charley."

So, I'm not proud of that part of my past. Charley insisted that we concentrate on the future. Wise, of course. Not always easy. And just the previous week, Michael, Charley's best friend from their Ivy League days, had insisted that we tie the knot at his ancestral estate in Connecticut. It had much to recommend it in terms of comfort and proximity to the City for guests—not that we would have more than a dozen or two. And it was the site of the first weekend trip that Charley and I shared.

It was kind of Michael to offer us his home. I wasn't certain if it had been his idea or if Rodney— my best friend and Michael's new husband—had come up with the idea. It was probably a case of "when inspiration strikes twice." It was a good idea. I could see that clearly.

Connecticut—why not? Michael is a gracious host, and Rodney would jump in and organize some seating—not to mention flowers and music—for the patch of grass at the bottom of the back lawn in front of the pool beneath the waterfall. It would be cool and lovely whatever the weather. And the Spirit of the Pool would surely watch over our nuptials.

That spring night, after Michael invited us to wed in Connecticut, we went to bed as usual. Even in the darkness Charley seemed to glow like burnished copper. And the moment I wrapped my arms around him, the furnace that powered Charley's precious body shared its warmth with me, as always, and filled me with safety and ease.

In the night, I had a dream about the Spirit. I had met him the previous July when he appeared to me, in the shower, at Michael's house. And again in the winter, I think it was, when he visited me in my lonely bed in Manhattan. There was no forgetting the Spirit's warm touch and his sweet voice. "You and Charley belong to me," he said. "Come home and let me bless your union."

I shouted or flinched or something, and then Charley and I were both wide awake. That's when we discovered that I had creamed all over Charley's ass. He chuckled, and he offered me a deep kiss. I guess I'll do just about anything for Charley's kiss. We quickly went back to sleep without bothering to clean up.

📖

"Peter, you asshole. What is wrong with you?" I asked myself that week. "It doesn't matter where you and Charley get married as long as it's legal and Charley is happy with it," I reminded myself. I tried to explain the situation to Rodney at lunch on Tuesday.

"Okay, Sweetie. You're talking to me, now," Rodney said. "What's going on?"

"I don't really know."

"Uh, huh. Let's get some truth going here," Rodney said. "Before you step up to the altar, you'd better step up to reality. Tell me what's happening, Peter. If you hide your feelings from me—and from yourself, for that matter—I can't help."

I wasn't certain I had any truth in me, but then it came to me, and I blurted it out: "All right, the truth is, I don't think I'm good enough for Charley. I'm afraid of ruining his life. Now, are you satisfied?"

"More like horrified," Rodney said.

"I love Charley so much it hurts, but so what? You of all people know. You know *best*, Rodney, what a failure I am at love. Look at me! I can't even keep it in my pants. What about Ajmal?"

"He never asked me to bed him, unfortunately, but I'd have said yes in a heartbeat. Why shouldn't you?"

"But Rodney, I was in love with Charley, and we had made ... promises by then. And yet, when some hot guy reached out to me, I was naked and on my back before I could finish his very good coffee—or tea, I think it was—that he offered me. In his huge apartment. With all the carpets and gilt furniture. And the silk bed linens. After lunch."

"Let's talk about promises, Sweetie. Did Charley ask you to wear a chastity belt while he was away?"

"No," I said. "In fact, I'm sure he said he didn't expect to return home to a saint. Or something like that."

"Did you ask Charley to be 'faithful' while he was away, whatever that means?"

"No, it never occurred to me to think about it. Charley told me he loves me. That was all I needed to know."

"And why do you suppose Charley loves you?" Rodney asked.

"I haven't a clue."

"Have you asked him why?"

"Uh, yes, actually," I replied.

"And?"

"He said I was his perfect mate. Or something like that. Or maybe that's what I said to him." I took a deep breath or two, and then I said, "Charley told me I complete him. He told me that I'm what has always been missing from his life. I'm sure he said that."

"Sounds right to me," Rodney said. "Smart man!"

"He also told me I make him feel sexy. Imagine that. The most exquisite man on Earth feels sexy when he's with me!"

"Peter, I can't believe we're having this conversation. After all these years. I'm only going to say this once. But I'm going to order a glass of wine first." Rodney flagged down our waiter and asked for two glasses of Oregon *pinot gris*. And two coffees and a check. We were on a business lunch hour, after all.

"Look, Peter," he said to me, "you don't seem to understand how precious you are. Some of us crave your friendship. There are people who value your business smarts, in case you haven't noticed. Could that be why you still have a decent job? Some of us fall hopelessly in love with you. But we all adore you. And everyone wants to be close to you. So let's cancel the pity party and get on with real life."

"Look, Rodney," I said, "since I brought up the topic of musical beds, what about Michael? Of course you knew, Roddy. And you're still speaking to me."

"Look, Sweetie, when we were dating, I was no more ready to commit to forever than you were. And as for Michael, I knew you were vetting him for me. And I'm glad you had a good time while you were doing it."

"You're a fucking saint, Rodney."

"More like a sinner, but at least I know who I am. Peter, you're the finest man I know, besides Michael. And the bravest. And the fact that you pushed Michael and me together makes me love you even more than I did back then—when we were just two boys together. Now let's do a reality check."

"That sounds dangerous," I said.

"Nevertheless. Peter, who loves you more than life itself—besides me, of course?"

"Charley does," I answered.

"And who wants to marry you as soon as possible?"

"Charley does," I had to answer.

"And who is dragging his feet for no good reason?" Rodney asked.

"I am," I admitted.

"And who is going to choose a wedding venue within the next forty-eight hours?" Rodney asked.

"I am," I said. And suddenly, it seemed possible.

The rest of the week felt lighter and less cluttered with negativity. Surely the springtime air had been softly scented by the blossoms bursting forth from flowering trees—for the previous week or two, anyway. I hadn't noticed. And yet I was suddenly aware of riots of color in every window box and tree box I passed in my travels through the city. I don't experience pollen allergies, so I was able to embrace the season totally.

Charley never pressed me for answers. He blessed me with his smile every morning, and he joined me in our bed every night. Most importantly, Charley made love to me. Often. And it was his *love* he shared. It oozed from every pore in his skin. The lust was nice too, but Charley's love bathed me with its purity and washed me clean. I had never thought much about baptism before Charley. And yet I had begun to crave the ritual of consecration that only he could administer. Daily, if at all possible.

It wasn't until the weekend—when Charley and I could share most of our time together without the distractions of business—that I was finally ready to make sense of the future. Charley suggested we take the 7 Train to one of the ethnic neighborhoods in Queens—there are dozens of them—where we could enjoy an early supper.

"I'm not pining to return to Singapore, Petey. Not without you, anyway. But the food is amazing. Let's see if we can find something like it in Queens. I think it's worth a shot."

"Of course, Darling," I said. So, we did a little online research and then headed out. Every moment with Charley was a new adventure, whether we were exploring the city or making love or shopping at Trader Joe's. Every moment. I knew it. I understood it for the first time. I sensed how precious our union had become. It was both thrilling and terrifying. I tried to focus on the thrills rather than the chills.

The restaurant Charley found for us was a narrow storefront, rather drab from the outside. Nothing visible from the street could predict the riot of exotic smells and voices that blasted the senses just inside the front door. It instantly made me think of my favorite Greek restaurant in Astoria, not because of the décor or the aromas or the sounds of the conversations, but merely because it was all about family.

Everyone in the place seemed to be celebrating relationships, whether they were grandparents or parents or children or grandchildren or maiden aunts or bachelor uncles or various combinations of the same. And where best to celebrate love? At table, of course! I was learning. Nothing in my childhood had prepared me for the intensity of family feelings. Nothing in my tentative adulthood—other than my honest love for Rodney—had suggested that I, too, could be part of a family.

And yet there I was, that soft spring evening, sitting across a tiny table from a glorious man who had asked me to join my life to his. We ordered the obligatory things: The fish head in red curry was amazingly good. The crab in a spicy sauce laced with chili oil was worth all the effort. There was a noodle dish, of course, and a jasmine rice cooked in coconut milk. All delicious. Durian was out of season, or unavailable, or something, so I was spared that.

Charley and I didn't speak much during dinner. Mostly we smiled. The depth of the flavors we shared demanded attention, and it would have been pointless to try to compete with the noise level in the room. After some very good tea, we strolled out onto the sidewalk and navigated slowly to the subway, just as all sated diners do.

"That was amazing," I said to Charley as we approached the train. "Would you be happy living in Singapore?"

"I'd be happy living anywhere with you, Peter. I thought you knew that." I stopped right there, on a sidewalk, in a Queens neighborhood I knew nothing about, and I threw my arms around Charley. He held me until I had recovered a bit. And then we continued our journey home.

It only occurred to me much later that no one who witnessed the silly faggot having a meltdown on a sidewalk in a neighborhood not his own that sweet April evening had seemed to notice the silly faggot's frailty nor to judge his right to it. Perhaps there's hope for the future of humanity after all.

As Charley and I were preparing for sleep that night, I decided I had delayed far too long. He had just brushed his teeth and was sliding into bed beside me when I said, "Why don't we shuffle off to Buffalo?"

"Excellent," Charley said. "Only I hear the Canadian side of the Falls is nicer. I did some homework, just in case. Getting married in Ontario is simple enough. We just have to hire someone to do the deed, buy a license, show up, say 'I do' in the right places, and then live the rest of our lives in wedded bliss. What do you think?"

"I think I may burst before we get there," I said.

"We can't have that," Charley said. "Ruptures are not allowed! Unless you develop a hernia, of course. That will be grandfathered in."

"Leave my grandfather out of this!" I said.

Charley said, "Sorry, but I'm taking on the whole fucking family, Peter. I want it all. Can you give me everything? I don't think I could bear to have less than all of you, Peter."

"Yes," I said. "Yes, Charley. I'll give you everything. And I want all of you. I haven't always known that. You've offered yourself to me, and I've made choices. À la carte. No more, Charley. I'm in."

We sealed our deal with a kiss, of course. Many of them. We didn't make love that night, oddly. It seemed too predictable. Sunday morning is really the best time for lovemaking, after all. Just before we fell asleep, I asked, "Will our friends forgive us if we disappear?"

"Eventually."

"They will, won't they!" I said. And then I was able to wrap myself around my perfect mate and settle in for the night. I'm sure I had been in a deep sleep for a few hours when I felt the Spirit of the Pool behind me, spooning me, just as surely as I was spooning Charley. The Spirit's warmth and sweetness felt at once familiar and exotic.

"What are you doing here?" I asked.

"I'm always here," he said. "Remember, you and Charley belong to me."

"I thought we belonged to each other," I said.

"That too," he said. "I'm looking forward to your wedding."

"Really?" I asked. "How will you find us?"

"That's easy," the Spirit said. "Your hearts will lead me."

"Even to Niagara Falls?"

"All true lovers are my responsibility," he said. "And so is every waterfall."

I wasn't even the least bit surprised. Maybe. I had assumed that Jesse would tell me, one day soon, that he wanted to add to our little family. But it was such a soft May evening, and I was so looking forward to a quiet supper without any drama. After a stressful week.

We were sitting in one of the new outdoor café spaces that sprang up during lockdown. It was one of the sensible ones that offer comfortable seating (with heat in the winter) that doesn't encroach on the needs of pedestrians or cyclists or drivers. Much. Tall order. Jesse looked so beautiful in the waning sunlight that I got a little misty. All right, a lot misty.

"David, are you okay?" he asked.

"Of course," I said. "Tell me more."

"Well, his parents are a really nice young couple who have to leave New York because the wife got a new posting in the Middle East, I think. The husband is a crypto trader, so he can work anywhere. They just can't see how they can take the baby with them."

"How old is he?"

"About a year and a half."

"Breed?" I asked.

"He's a poodle mix. So, you know he's super smart—and he won't shed. He's ginger-colored, I guess."

"If his coat is even remotely like the color of your pubes, Jesse, then I'll fall madly in love with him at first sight."

"David, I want this to be exactly what *you* want. I want it to be for *us*. I work with dogs every day. I don't need to take on a new responsibility unless it brings you joy."

"What's his name?"

"They call him Barkley. He'll adjust to a new name if you don't like that one."

"Jess, it's the boy's name. He's about to start a new life with new parents. The last thing he needs is something else new. Will you bring him home, or do you want me to stop by the kennel to meet him? He might hate me, of course."

"Impossible. David, do you really want this? If you don't, please tell me now."

"Love me, love my dog," I said. "Isn't that how it works?"

"Huh?"

"Never mind, Darling," I said. "That's an idiom from the history books you don't need to learn. Why don't you bring Barkley home with you tomorrow? This is exciting!" That was mostly the truth. I was so in love with Jesse that I would have welcomed his pet tarantula into our home. Fortunately, we didn't seem headed in that direction.

Jesse got up from his chair and came around the table to embrace me. I pressed my face to the sweetness of his slim belly and said, "Let's get some food into you. New daddies need to keep up their strength."

"I'll do most of the walking," Jesse said when he had returned to his chair and started to study the menu.

"Tell me what to get at the new pet food store on Third Avenue," I said. "I'll stop by tomorrow on my way home from work." And so it was pretty much a done deal.

⌸

"David, you'll make a great dog daddy," Harvey said to me at lunch the following Tuesday.

"I just want Jesse to be happy," I said.

"It's more than that, Darling," he said. "You're building a family."

"I suppose we are," I said. "And what about you and Jayden?"

"Yes, well, I promised him we could get a puppy—two puppies, most likely—as soon as his hours at the doggie center stabilize. I just don't want to get stuck with all the care. Or even worse, imagine if we have to hire a dog walker because Jayden is out at all hours caring for other people's pets."

"I hadn't thought of it that way," I said. "I don't know, Harve. They just love dogs so—our boys. It would seem cruel to deny them that. Jesse gives me everything, and he never asks for anything in return—except my love. He's very clear about wanting that. Sometimes I wonder why."

"Hush, Davey," he said. "Jesse worships you, because you're the only man in his life who offers him the emotional care and feeding he deserves. And that will never change. Now, order something to eat. We can't play hooky all afternoon."

As it happened, Barkley's parents weren't quite ready to give him up, so he didn't come to live with us until the following week. I was fine with the delay. It gave me time to accept—mostly—the notion of adding to our little family group. Was I prepared to open my heart and find love for another creature? I hoped so.

For the first decades of my life, Harvey was the only person I loved. No one in my childhood—other than a kindergarten teacher and my friend Ben's mother—had modeled what it's like to be a loving person. If she and her husband hadn't taken me in when life at home became unbearable.... I wasn't exactly a street kid when I came to New York. I had studied at a community college while working long hours in low-paying jobs to survive. And then came the scholarship and the business degree that let me start a real life.

So I knew how to play the game. But I always felt a little bit emotionally on the edge. Other than my very real feelings for Harvey—which I seemed unable to honor as I might have, when we met—I wondered if I had the ability to love, really. Until Jesse came along. And suddenly, a kid who was both fucked-up and wise beyond his tender years taught my heart everything it needed to learn. Maybe.

Surely parenting would teach us new *together* skills. Surely we would grow closer as a result. Surely I had no idea what I was doing. Building a family. What did I know about that? Nothing. Jesse, I reminded myself, had more real experience of family than I did.

I didn't envy Jesse's experience of childhood, of course. But maybe, just a tiny bit, I envied that he grew up with a father who loved him. The fact that

Jesse's loving father also fucked him threw lots of shade on the notion of paternal love. But I had moments—my darkest ones, most likely—when I almost yearned for that kind of connection rather than the indifference that had been my experience of family.

All deep in the past, of course. And yet, all a part of the fabric of our current lives. At dinner that night, I said to Jesse, "Does Barkley have balls?"

"He does, actually. He has a pedigree, so his parents wanted to reserve the right to breed him. And he has a sweet nature, so there was never a need to improve his behavior. Hormonally. Why do you ask?"

"It's hard to say, but we've all been told to edit ourselves so often. And I guess I hoped that our new son could be gloriously himself without alteration."

"I never thought of it that way, Davey, but you're right," Jesse said. And he kissed me. Jesse's kiss had become so precious to me in the months we had been together. Since mid-July. Not even a full year. Some years are different from others, I surmised. Some years plod by as if we are in a haze. And we're left with thoughts like "Did I really do that?" and "What was that summer about?"

Not my almost-year with Jesse. Every moment made me tingle. Every hour had surprise in it. Every day dawned with a new sense of promise. In short, I was terrified! Nothing in my past had prepared me for the possibility of real happiness. And yet I had found it. But could I keep it?

"I need your help," Harvey said to me at lunch on Friday. "Jayden's birthday is coming up next week, and I can't figure out what to get him. And don't tell me to get him a puppy. That is not going to happen this year."

"How about a gold cock ring?" I suggested.

"Davey, no one can afford that much gold. I think you've seen what Jayden is carrying."

"Only once, and from a distance, Harve," I said, "but I see your point. Don't worry, Darling. I'll help you think of the perfect gift."

"Well, speaking of puppies, and new families, I'll bet your new son could stay with Jayden and me when you and Jesse go away this summer," Harvey said. "I think he'd be happier with us than at the kennel. And it would give me a chance to ease into the notion of doggie care."

"That's very generous of you, Harve," I said. "Sounds perfect. By the way, I can't tell you how happy it makes me to see you in love. I always wanted that for you. Especially since I was so bad at it—at showing you my love. But never mind the past. Jayden is a very lucky man."

"I think I'm the lucky one. But forget that. What am I going to get him for his birthday?"

"We'll think of the perfect gift," I said, and I headed back to the office. I was glad of business responsibilities. They took my mind off building a new family and trying to be a good friend. Briefly, anyway. Just long enough for me to yearn to be a partner again. And a parent. And a pal.

📖

"Didn't I tell you what a sweetheart he is?" Jesse asked as he took Barkley off lead and allowed him to bound into the apartment and throw himself at me. I received Barkley's attention easily, and I returned it with natural affection. We sized each other up instantly.

"Well, Beauty," I said as I fluffed his coat and accepted Barkley's kisses—all but the ones headed directly for my mouth—"welcome to your new home!" As if on cue, he let out a load bark that I took to be like a child's whoop of joy—as much as I know anything about childhood, having skipped much of it.

Barkley knew Jesse by heart, of course, and once he was satisfied that he had cracked my code, he began to explore the apartment. Fortunately, I don't collect fragile art glass or other breakables. So we let him roam—bounce really—until he was satisfied with his tour.

Jesse went to the kitchen to start dinner. I poured us a glass of wine. Barkley joined us, fresh from his travels, and settled at Jesse's feet, awaiting further instructions. Barkley looked just as he had looked before his adventure began, except that he was carrying my rubber ducky in his mouth. Harvey gave it to me when we were dating, and I had always kept it on the edge of the tub in my bathroom.

"Ducky has a new owner," I said. "I don't think Harvey will mind if I pass him on to baby."

"Squeak," said Ducky. The dog gave his second bark of approval of the day. But his cry was a bit muffled that time, for fear of losing the new prize, I assumed.

"Daddy David wants to speak to you, Barkley," Jesse said. "Go to him." Obediently, Barkley left the safety of Jesse's orbit and followed me into the living room. When I sat on the sofa, Barkley bounded up on my lap, carefully placed Ducky between his front paws, and gazed intently into my eyes.

And so, of course, I told Barkley all those silly things that doggie daddies tell their babies—about how thrilled I was that he had come to live with us and that we intended to love him and protect him to the very best of our abilities. He listened patiently to every word—always making eye contact—until I had run out of foolishness to share. I had no doubt that he understood every word I spoke to him.

A quick kiss to my chin and Barkley settled in on my lap to resume his getting-to-know-you session with Ducky. When Jesse looked in on us, to give us an update on dinner time, Barkley and I no doubt presented a perfect picture of domestic harmony.

Over supper, I asked Jesse, "What do you think Jayden would most like for his birthday? Harvey wants to get it right, and I promised to help. I know you don't see as much of Jay as you used to, now that you're taking classes, but I figured you'd know."

"Interesting question. You know, Jayden is actually a serious guy," Jesse said.

"I don't doubt that."

"No, I just mean he has his priorities straight. He knows things are good for him right now: he has a job and a place to live and the love of a good man. The same as I do, actually. There isn't much more to want."

I jumped up from the table and lunged for Jesse, pressing him to my heart. "Please never make me any happier than I am this minute," I said.

"No promises," he said. I tore myself away from Jesse and returned to my dinner. Barkley satisfied himself that nothing of real drama was happening between the daddies and then settled back into his squeaky love affair with Ducky.

"You asked about Jayden," Jesse said. "I think his biggest concern right now is his grandmother. She's the only one who ever looked after him, and she lives alone, and she's kind of isolated where she is. He can't get up to the Bronx that often to visit her, so he worries."

"How old is she?" I asked.

"I don't know, in her sixties, I guess." Jesse added, "I think her health is mostly pretty good, but Jayden says she's alone too much. And it takes her long bus rides just to find fresh food, so she doesn't always bother when she's only cooking for herself."

"I don't know what Harvey can do about that," I said, "but I'll work on it." I did, actually. I pondered Jayden's situation and wondered how Harvey might help. Mostly, though, I rejoiced in my own happiness.

📖

"Davey, I had a fantastic idea for Jayden's birthday," Harvey said to me at lunch on Monday.

"Really? What did you come up with?"

"Well, you know we spent Thanksgiving—and Christmas—with Jayden's grandmother, Florence. He adores her, and he's concerned about her living alone, now that he's in Manhattan. Jay's mother was pretty much worthless as a parent, so Florence stepped in and raised him. I'm going to invite her to come and live with us."

"What!"

"It makes perfect sense, David. The second bedroom is empty. It's small, but it has its own bathroom. There's a senior center two blocks away, so she can do things and make new friends if she wants to. There are plenty of food markets nearby, if she wants to cook. David, she's a terrific cook! But most of all, I think it would make Jay very happy. And that's my first priority."

"Harvey, you amaze me every moment," I said. "I don't know what I was thinking all those years ago when I let you get away."

"You were thinking about the future, of course, Davey. You were waiting for your perfect mate to come along. And he did."

"Looks like we're both building new families," I said. "Only slightly different."

"Not so different," Harvey said. "Jayden tells me that Florence loves dogs. Well, I'm getting ahead of myself: I haven't even asked Florence to live with us—yet. But if she wants to help out with daytime walks and such, then Jay and I might become doggie daddies sooner than I thought!"

Saying goodbye to Sean before leaving for the airport was painful indeed. It was a Sunday morning. In mid-March, I guess. That whole late winter/early spring is something of a jumble in my mind. All I wanted was the chance to cement my new relationship with the glorious man who had come to live with me. What I got was a business trip to Texas.

True, Sean wanted to come with me. But I couldn't let him delay his studies. I knew, from the bottom of my heart, that he would make a great mental health counselor/social worker. I knew that he would bring clarity and comfort to countless trans kids—in particular—who were struggling with life. Who was I to put my needs above theirs?

"When is Mikey coming?" I asked.

"Alex, he's moving in this evening, after work," Sean said. "You know that." I did, of course. I was glad Sean's best friend had agreed to live with him while I was away. Knowing that Sean would have company made me feel less guilty about rooming with Rory in Houston.

"I hate packing," I said as I was trying to choke down a few sips of coffee and half a blueberry muffin. "I'm always certain I've forgotten something, and then I always end up carrying more than I need. How could you love such a freak!"

"Hush, Alex," Sean said. "You're thorough. And careful. The same as when you make love to me. That's why you're the only man I want. Now, two more pairs of socks and then close the fucking bag." I did as I was told. Sean was wearing the rainbow silk robe I had given him. When his body moved, the fabric slid over his creamy skin like a monarch butterfly's wing caressing a milkweed pod. I had sworn not to get crazy that Sunday morning. So much for promises.

We hefted my bag and my carry-on to the front door, and then I took Sean's hand and led him to the sofa. He sat, obediently, and allowed me to kneel before him. Then I parted the fabric that separated me from everything I really wanted, and I planted my face in the middle of the sweetness and warmth between Sean's legs.

How would I survive a couple of months without that feast? How, indeed! It was getting late. Rory would be arriving in an Uber in a few minutes, surely. But Sean did not resist my needs. He held my face gently while I explored him. Had there been time, I would have gladly stripped and topped Sean with all the passion of the night before. More, really, since it was something of a last time. The last, but only just for now, surely. May would come soon enough. May and reunion.

When Sean began to shout, I knew that he was giving me his best. It would have to hold me for a while. We were still panting when Rory texted to tell me he was downstairs. "Let me get a towel," Sean said. He quickly wet a dishtowel in the kitchen and bathed my face. And then it was a quick kiss, luggage, and out the door.

I found Houston welcoming enough. It was the tail end of winter, technically, and yet the heat and humidity were rolling in already. I was glad that I would be home in NYC by summer. New York summers can be brutal, of course, but at least there are lots of parks and leafy glades where breezes and sometimes fountains cool the body at least partially. *Winds*, I should say, rather than *breezes*, now that wind is the new normal.

I didn't much want to be in Houston, but at least the project was something to be proud of. The renderings looked great—not just the ones I had been directly involved with—but pictures always look promising. It isn't until you're actually standing in the space itself that the project comes alive—or doesn't.

The site had a ... a sense of place, I guess I have to say. Yes, it would welcome millions of theatergoers in years to come. Yes, the luxury apartments on the high floors would have delicious views of the bay. Yes, the "affordable" housing would be comfortable and convenient. Public transportation? Check. Trader Joe's *and* Whole Foods? Check. Public spaces for all seasons with lots of room for art and family outings? Check.

A few days into our stay, when Rory and I had begun to feel we really understood the project, Rory said, "This is the best decision your firm has made since they decided to hire you, Alex."

"Thanks, Darling," I said, "but hiring *you* is always their best choice. That atrium will be breathtaking once you've finished with the plantings."

"Yes, well, I hope you're right. Anyway, we need to keep up our strength. How about I take you to dinner tonight? Some place nice? I'm bored with the local eats already."

"Sure," I said.

"Give me a minute to text that cute liaison guy. He'll have some restaurant suggestions." Yes, the guy was cute indeed, and yes, he suggested a place that sounded promising. So we primped a bit, changed into clean shirts, and headed out to an early dinner.

The restaurant—something about Grace, I think—was spacious in a way that New York restaurants rarely are and welcoming in the way that all great eateries are. The hostess seated us at a table that felt both central to all the action and warmly intimate.

It's a paradox probably only noticed by people who are involved with architecture and interior design. Hospitality presents challenges unknown to other arts. Maybe. Rory and I didn't discuss it, but I'm sure we both realized, from the moment the hostess seated us, that we would dine well—no matter what.

As it happened, we arrived just before the end of Oyster Happy Hour. So that put me in a positive frame of mind all out of proportion to the comfort of our seating arrangement. "Will you share a *plateau* with me?" I asked Rory.

"Of course, Alex," he said. "Perfect!" So, we were able to place our order just before 6:00. There was also a wine special, so we selected a perfectly pleasant bubbly—cava or prosecco, as I remember. And within twenty minutes we were presented with a great tower of iced seafood: dozens of plump, briny oysters, of course; jumbo Gulf shrimp, of course—the fresh ones for a change; blue crab in several formats (always a great favorite of mine); and a very handsome split lobster on the top tier.

"I wish Sean were here," I said.

"So do I," Rory said. "I want my best friend completely happy."

"You've noticed, haven't you?"

"Yes, Alex," he said. "I've never seen you completely happy before now. I always wanted that for you. Never could seem to give it. Now you've found the man of your dreams. I'm glad I helped." Rory had indeed helped, of course. He had vetted Sean for me. And he had introduced us.

"You're a remarkable man, Rory," I said. "And you like oysters. I guess that makes you just about perfect." It had been all about lust—the night that Rory brought Sean to my apartment. Two buddies with an insatiable appetite for each other plus a tasty newbie to fill the sandwich. All lust to start, true, but the persistent tingle that followed was maybe even more about romance.

I couldn't help smiling—grinning, most likely—as I sat across from my best friend and enjoyed an abundance of my favorite food. Did I eat too much? Of course! Did I regret my overindulgence? Not for an instant. When we got back to the apartment—still a little giddy in the aftermath of good food, good drink, and good company—Rory said, "Will you sleep with me tonight, Alex? I don't feel like being alone."

"Of course," I said. "I'll just brush my teeth." Yes, I would gladly sleep with Rory. I would do anything he asked of me. Most likely. Hadn't he comforted me those long nights the previous fall after Sean walked out on me? Hadn't Rory held me and kept me safe from heartbreak all through the night? I got myself ready for sleep and headed to Rory's room.

He looked so sweet lying there on several plumped-up pillows, watching Netflix with his tortoise-rimmed glasses on. One might almost forget that Rory is the most dangerously sexual man God ever created—according to everyone who has ever known him, anyway. Without really looking away from the screen, he flipped back the covers and gestured to me to join him. I obeyed.

Rory leaned over and kissed me, then he refocused on the series he was watching. "Are you okay with this?" he asked. "It's only another fifteen minutes."

"Of course." I loved being close to Rory, just as always. A decade and a half since we first met, wasn't it? And my delight in his company was unabated and unabashed. When the series episode ended, Rory removed his glasses, stowed them on the night table, and turned off the TV and his bedside lamp. As he settled in, Rory took my left arm and drew it around his torso.

"Thanks, Alex," he said.

"For?"

"For letting me love you." I didn't have an answer for that. I did, however, have a response to holding Rory's perfect, warm body close to mine. His scent filled my nostrils, and I went into full erection mode. No surprise there. Being close to Rory always had that effect. I wondered how different my life might be if Rory had let me spoon him every night. Every night for fifteen years. I couldn't do the math in my head. Not that the numbers mattered. Missed opportunities are mere nothingness, after all. Why quantify them?

"Sleep well, my friend," I said. "I love you, too." Had I ever said that before? Once or twice, perhaps. The previous autumn. When Rory got me through Sean's absence. I did love Rory, of course. I suppose I had loved him all those years without really being aware. I should have known: celebrating his body had always been an act of pure devotion, as much a spiritual ecstasy as it was an explosion of sensual pleasure. Hmmm. Could this be love?

It was a quiet night. Dreamless, as I remember. I settled into my role—my single responsibility: my sole purpose on Earth that night was to hold Rory and keep him safe. The morning light brought not just the promise of a new day and a magpie's call, but also the realization that I had performed my duty.

I disentangled my body from Rory's as gently as possible. He stirred slightly but then settled back to sleep. I couldn't help noticing the faint smile on his face. I wondered if it had anything to do with me. In all the years that we had bounced around beds—his or mine—we had rarely slept. So I couldn't be sure about anything as domestic as a sleeping smile.

I was making coffee when Rory wandered into the kitchen looking sweetly disheveled and sporting glorious morning wood. He looked like a little boy, really—a little boy with a huge cock, of course. The morning sunlight glinted off the delicate chain around his neck. I hadn't noticed it when we went to bed, and yet he probably wore it always—ever since I chose it for him as a rare birthday gift.

I wondered what Rory had ever given me—besides his devotion and more exquisite orgasms than one man could possibly deserve. Some theater tickets, and a little gold heart keychain, for certain. Our relationship had never been about things. Instead, it was a smile, a touch, a taste, and everything else those shared experiences led to. Rory walked over to the stove and kissed me, then he planted his arms around my shoulders. "Thank you," he said.

"For?"

"For making breakfast, of course. What time is the meeting with the City Council representative?"

"It's at 10:00," I said. "We have plenty of time. How do you feel about grits?"

"As a foodstuff or as a cultural icon?"

"As a foodstuff," I said. "I'm making some. I think it takes twenty minutes."

"Sounds delicious," Rory said with good-natured skepticism. "I'll take a shower." I tweaked Rory's cock—still impressive even after its morning glory had started to fade. He gave me a sweet kiss and headed off to his bathroom.

The workday unfolded smoothly. The City of Houston seemed to be supportive of the project Rory and I were directing. No doubt they would have preferred to use local design talent, and yet it always pays to get the very best! And there was no doubt in my mind that my team—plus Rory—was creating the ideal cultural and residential center for that space in that city at that moment in time.

It was amazing to me how Rory navigated the politics of business. He always seemed to operate from a position of quiet strength—and total competence. Not so different from his approach to the bedroom, I realized. He had nothing to hide and nothing to prove. I envied his confidence, I suppose. Even more than that, I think, I valued his high opinion of me.

If Rory hadn't adored my body all these years, would I feel desirable? I have a mirror. I know what I look like. I'm fine with that. I go to the gym. I keep fit. I've bedded every man I've ever really wanted to bed (plus dozens I didn't much want to, of course). But it suddenly occurred to me, far from home, in a strange city where the air was different, the sunlight was different, and the water tasted different, that Rory was the first man who made me feel beautiful.

And we're not just talking about the first fuck, here. Every moment spent with Rory, through the years, had been like that. Was there no one else? I thought I had found it with Ben. I was willing to give Rory up for nearly five years because I thought Ben adored me as much as I adored him. But when Ben's heart went off on a Southern tangent, I realized that I had gotten it wrong.

I was too wounded—and embarrassed, probably—to reach out to Rory after Ben followed his new love to New Orleans. It was Rory who reached out to me. We had a mutual friend or two, after all. Someone knew I was suddenly single. Someone told Rory, surely. And then he reappeared in my life at the very moment I needed him most.

And then Rory brought Sean to me. And then I thought my life was set. And then Sean left me in

the fall. And then he came back at New Year's. Melodrama, anyone? It felt neither lightweight nor silly
at the time. It felt like the highest stakes imaginable.
It felt like life and death. Did Sean make me feel
beautiful? Yes. More than that, I think, he made me
feel the need to be accountable.

All the years that I had bedded Rory and worshiped his body—the first decade, anyway—it had
never occurred to me that he needed me for anything
other than the pleasure my body could offer his.
There was something about falling in love with Ben
that changed all that. There was something so painful about giving Rory up. I guess it showed me how
much Rory and I needed each other.

And then Sean entered my life and changed everything. Nearly. But I was aware that I still needed
Rory in my life. Surely that was healthy. Falling in
love doesn't mean giving up friends and family. But
does it mean giving up extra-relationship lust? Probably. I had assumed I would again give Rory up. But
not as I had given him up in the years I was with
Ben. This time I would keep his friendship. This
time I would keep wholeness in my life. I would
merely lose the need to worship Rory's perfect body.
On a regular basis. Tall order.

That strange spring, in a strange city, the high
point of my day was always my video call with Sean.
His face glowed with ginger sweetness. His smile
warmed my heart and assured me I was doing the
right thing. Over the weeks, I watched his beard
grow out and then experience a major trim. I eagerly
listened to his college news and bits and pieces about
New York life that didn't warrant attention in the
Texas press. And I yearned to hold Sean close all
through the night. And then I got myself ready for

bed in the alien space that was mine to occupy for a season. And then there was Rory.

One evening, in the second week of our stay, I think, Rory called me to his bedroom and said, "I think this bed is better than the one in your room, Alex. Why don't you join me?"

"Sure," I said. I didn't know what else to say. Did the invitation apply just to that night? Or did Rory mean that the two of us should share his bed every night for the rest of our stay in Houston? I wasn't certain. I got ready for sleep and then returned to Rory's room.

Just as in the aftermath of our oyster extravaganza, Rory was looking very cute, tucked into his bed, bare-chested (and bare everywhere else under the covers) watching a TV series through the lenses in his heavy-framed eyeglasses. As before, Rory beckoned me to join him, so I dropped my robe and slipped in beside him. He drew me close, and we watched the rest of the show with my head resting next to his.

"Are you sleepy?" he asked when the show ended. "I can find something else if you want."

"No, I think I'm ready to turn in," I said. "We have to be rested when we meet the Parks Commissioner tomorrow."

"You're right, Alex. I'm going to pour a cognac. You'll join me?"

"Sure." Rory slipped out of bed and headed for the kitchen. I got to see first the perfection of his backside and then the perfection of his frontside as he returned with our drinks. I had memorized every square inch of Rory's body over the years, and yet everything seemed different in that blandly comfy rental apartment in a city I doubted I would ever learn.

We sipped our drinks and chatted briefly about the design project. And then it was time for lights out. As before—on oyster night—Rory reached for my arm and drew it around him. And as we eased into the pose, I soaked up his warmth and his scent. But there was nothing relaxing in that arrangement of limbs. Instead, I began to quiver with desire. All over. My intense erection, reaching for the magnificence of Rory's ass, was almost the least of it.

I knew that if I shifted my grip on Rory's tight torso I would discover a matching example of full-blown masculinity. I didn't dare go there. It wasn't where we were supposed to be headed. Was it? Surely Rory and I were no longer lovers. Surely that part of my life belonged to Sean. Surely I had no idea how to deal with my feelings.

"Rory," I whispered.

"Hush, Alex," he said. "It's late." I couldn't argue with that. I did as I was told.

◫

The days that followed became rather routine. Daytime meetings, visits to the construction site, phone calls with city officials, little fires to extinguish. And every evening I had my video chat with Sean. At first, the chat was always followed by dinner with Rory. And then bedtime. With Rory.

But at some point in the third week, Rory started dating the cute liaison boy. The one who recommended the oyster restaurant. He had a name, of course. Ken. He looked like a Ken. I'm certain under other circumstances I might have found him adorable. But since he had captured much of Rory's time and attention, I could only associate Ken with isolation and loneliness. You don't suppose there was a measure of jealousy there, do you?

Ken began to sleep over—in Rory's bed, of course—and I returned to my original room. Did I often lie in bed, masturbating and wishing I were part of the action in the next room? You bet I did! But most of the time I did my work and chatted with Sean every evening and got a good night's sleep in air-conditioned comfort.

One morning, I was making coffee while Rory joined me in the kitchen and Ken was taking a shower. I probably resented the fact that mornings with Rory were no longer mine alone. Rory looked just as cute and silly as ever, with his hair all over his head and his easy nakedness and his delicious sexuality on view. Both of us had probably acquired a bit of a face tan. Other than that, we were unchanged. Except for Ken.

"Ken thinks you're really hot," Rory said.

"Really?"

"Obviously, he has good taste. Ken wants to go to bed with you," Rory said as I handed him a cup of coffee.

"That's nice," I said, buttering some toast.

"It could be you and Ken, or maybe the three of us? I don't know, Alex. You don't talk to me much these days. I don't know what you want."

"That makes two of us," I said. "Could we maybe talk about this tonight? Or some time when Ken isn't here and you're free?"

"Of course, Buddy," he said. Ken walked in, still a little damp from his shower, just as gloriously naked as Rory was, obviously having taken his behavior cues from his host. Ken's front view was easy on the eyes: tight little torso, long legs, and a medium-gauge Prince Albert ring bouncing at the end of his pretty cock. I poured Ken some coffee and indicated the toast and jam, Greek yoghurt, and boiled eggs on the counter.

"Thanks, Alex," he said, and he gave me a warm smile, a bit of a hug, and a peck on the cheek. Did I mind that Ken's right hand strayed below my waist when he embraced me? Not at all. It was a slight, casual gesture. A quick meeting of manhoods as he drew my body to his. I almost wished that we were not separated by a thin layer of blue cotton. But if I had had the slightest intention of dropping my robe, that was not the moment for it.

Rory gave me his familiar glance-over-the-rim-of-his-glasses, even though he didn't happen to be wearing them. I busied myself with straightening up the breakfast things. "Okay, Growing Boy," Rory said to Ken. "Grab something to eat. We have to get dressed and out of here." Ken obediently took what he wanted and headed to Rory's bedroom.

Rory and I both watched Ken as he walked away. An exceptionally well-made ass, surely. And the bird-of-paradise tattooed on his left cheek said it all. Rory gave me a kiss. "Thanks, Alex," and he tweaked my cock. "Glad to feel signs of life." And then he was off to get ready for the workday.

I *was* showing signs of life, after all, beneath the little robe I had bought for the trip. I had been accustomed to frequent orgasms throughout my adulthood (such as it's been). Daily? Usually. Even more frequently? At times. Rory had shared so much of that energy with me through the years. Ben, of course. But I had begun to wonder if Ben was much more than a blip on my radar. And then Sean appeared, and I wanted every bit of my erotic energy to be his.

But there I was, in Houston, Texas, of all places, without Sean, and without the physical comfort I craved. And there was nothing available even from my best friend—the man who knew my body better than I did and still found me desirable. After all these years. So, if at times I seemed to be thinking with my dick instead of my brain, then it's just sort of a boy thing. And I will only apologize up to a point.

I was uncertain, indeed, about how the rest of my stay in Houston might unfold. Days were about responsibility and careful competence. But nights were about wild imaginings and loneliness bordering on despair. True, Sean would come to visit—in just over two weeks. But what would he find when he arrived? What would be left of me? Would I be love-able? Would I be worthy of him?

A couple of evenings later, Ken couldn't come to the apartment with Rory after work. He had to help his mother with something or other. Mostly I was happy to have Rory to myself. And I was pleased to have an evening free of the question of whether or not I intended to have sex with Ken. I had been avoiding that decision for a few days, and I disliked the air of anticipation that enveloped the three of us.

"Will you have dinner with me?" I asked Rory as we were traveling "home."

"Of course," he said. "How about barbecue?"

"Sure," I said. We dropped off our briefcases and changed into Ts and shorts. "Just let me call Sean," I said. I needed that lifeline. Did it anchor me to reality? I hoped so. "Hi, Beauty," I said when Sean answered my call. "I missed you today. Same as every day!" Mikey moved into the camera frame. A cute boy, for sure, though his new goatee looked a bit silly. Mikey greeted me, and he asked after Rory. I assured the two of them that I would deliver their greetings to Rory, and then it was time to sign off. I began to wonder if those moments of long-distance sanity were helping or hurting my mental health.

The restaurant—which Ken had recommended, of course—was within walking distance of the apartment. It was a pleasant evening. A bit less sultry than usual. I was glad to have Rory's undivided attention. His dark eyes sparkled across the table from me. The strength of his jawline, the not-quite-wholesome warmth of his smile, and the curve of his biceps all contributed to the rumble in my crotch.

The noise level in the dining room was fairly high, lending the well-known false sense of intimacy that diners enjoy. As always, when we ate together, Rory would occasionally place his hand on the table, palm up, beckoning me to meet him in the middle. And I always did. Even in cowboy country. Or were all these locals oilmen? It didn't seem to matter. The food was flavorful—and abundant—and the beer was cold.

When we strolled back to the apartment that evening, I was not as relaxed as I had hoped to be, considering that Rory and I had enjoyed a pleasant evening together and might still have shared time ahead of us. Intimate time, even. But nothing seemed to be enough. I had begun to ache. That was it.

The ache that had started in my heart had spread throughout my body. Especially to my crotch. I ached for physical contact with a man. Did I want Rory? Of course. Did I want Ken? Probably. Would I have preferred both of them at the same time? Likely. Maybe I only really wanted Sean, but Sean was 1,400 miles away. And I was feeling desperate.

"Will you sleep with me tonight?" Rory asked.

"Sure," I said. So, I brushed my teeth, went over my schedule for the next day, and then headed to Rory's room. He turned off his TV, stowed his glasses on the night table, and pulled back the covers for me. I dropped my robe and joined him. Rory didn't relax into our proximity any more than I did. I could feel his gaze. And I knew he was waiting for information.

"Rory, I need to ask you some questions," I said. "I need some answers."

"Fire away, Captain," he said.

"Rory, do you love me?"

"Yes. Always have. Always will. Why do you ask?"

"Because I'm desperate over here," I said. "I don't know what I'm doing. I want Sean so badly that it's driving me crazy, and yet, if you don't make love to me, tonight, I may die. My heart may just stop fucking beating. Is that possible?"

Rory wrapped his arms around me and said, "Yes, Alex, I believe it is possible to die from a lack of love. But it's not going to happen here. Not tonight. Because the love I feel for you is complete and forever. So you're safe from cardiac complications."

"I feel the same way about you, Rory," I said, "but how can I also want Sean so desperately? And a little

Ken on the side would be fun, too. But I won't push it."

"You're a man, Alex. A very beautiful man. An honest man. And you have the biggest heart on the planet. There's room for all of us in it. Don't fight it. It's your greatest strength."

Well, I had no fight left in me. Not that evening, anyway. Perhaps I would make better sense of my life later on. With Sean in my arms. In my own bed. In the city that felt like mine. But that April night, in an alien landscape, I embraced my best friend and welcomed the healing power of his love.

Tale Number Six

Izzy asked me to have lunch with him on a Wednesday in April. We hadn't seen much of each other over the winter, so I was delighted to have him all to myself for an hour or two. I sat across from my best friend at a little neighborhood Italian place we had frequented back when we were dating. How long had I loved him unconditionally? Probably fifteen years. It felt like a lifetime in some ways. But in other ways, it felt like we had only just met.

I admired Izzy's inky black hair and his perfect skin. The little divot between his collar bones peeked out from the top of his shirt, anchoring the sweep of masculinity that was his throat. Izzy's smile dazzled just as it always had. His dark eyes sparkled and smoldered, as always. And when he took my hand, did I feel a great swell in my crotch? Of course. Just as always. "Beau, I need your help," he said when we had ordered a plate of pasta and some red wine.

"You have it."

"Roger says he's in love with me."

"Well, of course he's in love with you," I said, secretly pleased with the success of my first real attempt at matchmaking. "You're the most loveable man on Earth, Izzy. Everyone is in love with you."

"Could we maybe get just a little bit serious?" he asked.

"This *is* serious," I said. "I don't take love lightly any more than you do. What's the issue?"

"Beau, Roger says he loves me and he wants to join his life to mine. He says he thinks we should live together. He hasn't mentioned marriage, but I think it's only a matter of time before he goes there."

"Izzy, how do you feel about him?"

"I adore him, Beau. He's the only man—besides you—I ever wanted so completely. He's sweet, he's sexy, he tastes great, he smells like a corner of heaven, he's funny, he's sunny, and he loves me, Beau. He's given me his heart."

"So, where's the problem?" I asked.

Izzy looked at me with real terror in his gaze. "I don't know if I can do it," he said. "*You* offered me a chance like this, and you'll remember how I fucked it up. How can I expect to get it right this time?"

"Oh, so that's what this is about," I said. "Okay, Izzy, I have some thoughts. Here goes: First of all, *we* were a long time ago. The streams we stepped into then have long since flowed to the sea. True, you didn't want what I wanted then. But if I had been smart—if I had been able to trust the wisdom of my heart—I would have won you. I would have convinced you to give me a chance to prove that I could love you completely for the rest of my life."

I can't say which of us was more shaken by my declaration. The pasta arrived just then, so we could accept grated cheese and freshly ground pepper while we tried to gather our thoughts. A few bites, a sip of wine, a smile, and it was time to return to the matter at hand. I decided the ball was still in my court:

"First, I'm sure you know that I *will* love you completely for the rest of my life, Izzy. It's just more of a long-distance relationship than I had in mind. But the important thing here is that we weren't ready then. Nothing to do with who got it right and who got it wrong. I wasn't ready until last July when I found Bradley in my arms and I suddenly knew that I didn't want to live without him beside me. And you weren't ready until recently when Roger kissed you and reminded you of the possibility of bliss."

It was exhausting, really. Izzy looked a bit wiped out, too. Probably the best investment counselor and one of the toughest businessmen I've ever known was no match for the intricacies of the heart. He had asked for my help, after all, so I couldn't just leave it there.

"Do it, Iz," I said. "Give Roger that big, beautiful heart of yours. As well as your big, beautiful cock. He'll prize every part of you. Go out on a limb, Darling. You know I'll catch you if you fall. I think you also know that Roger is worth the risk."

Izzy was quiet until we were sipping espresso, and then he said, "I thought I could live without a partner, Beau. I thought that my work and a few precious friends completed my life. And they did. Until you threw Roger at me."

"You threw Bradley at me," I said. It was true, of course. We laughed freely, and it broke the tension of the last half hour. I said, "You know, by the way, if Roger hurts you, I'll tear him into shreds and feed him to the fish. We're surrounded by very healthy waterways these days. Lots of mouths to feed. He'll be lunch and done. Just saying."

"That's comforting to know. I guess. If you think I can do this, Beau, then I'm going to give it my best."

"Good," I said. "Will you share a *tiramisu*?" And that's how I learned that we had both moved on. Finally. My best friend and I had both done some growing up. And both in the same year!

📖

"Just when I thought it couldn't get any better, it did," I said. Bradley tightened his grip on my torso. Perhaps we were both hoping that I could share the precious warmth of his interior indefinitely. I know that was my goal. He seemed to want it, too.

Bradley said, "You give me everything I need, Daddy." By way of reply I pressed my mouth to his, and I drank in his sweetness. Heady stuff—kisses like that. A complete sex act in miniature. Maybe. Or a declaration of love. Sometimes. Lust is nice, too. I prefer a package deal. That is exactly what Bradley had given me since July.

It seemed a shame to have to stir from our embrace. But the stiffest cock loses its starch eventually; folks gotta pee; and Sunday breakfast demands attention. The fact that I only had Bradley all to myself every other Sunday made each moment extra precious. We launched our day with lots of smiles and embraces and the occasional kiss.

"Talk to me, Baby," I said, as we made coffee and soft-boiled eggs. "I miss you so much—most of the week. I feel like I don't know enough about what's happening to you and how you're feeling."

"I know, Daddy," he said. "Nina and I get so busy with our clients and our plans for the business that I sometimes wonder what I'm doing. All I really want is to be with you." That earned him a very deep kiss, of course.

"I know, Baby," I said. "But this is not forever: the separation part, I mean. The together part *is* forever." That earned *me* a very deep kiss. "What does Nina say about your progress?"

"She believes we're on track to build a viable business by the end of next year. She thinks health and fitness are always the future. I agree. Personal Fitness has to be scalable, of course. It has to function with only the *idea* of Nina and me attached to it, instead of our constant presence. Gerald thinks we're on our way. Izzy agrees."

"Speaking of Izzy," I said, "you know he talked to me about Roger."

"I don't see that much of Roger, since he's Nina's client, really, but I can tell how happy he looks. And I can tell you how happy it makes *me* to know that my Daddy looks out for his friends."

"Yes, well, I'm not so sure about that, but I think we're all finding gold nuggets in our pans this year. Izzy told me he and Roger are in love. I couldn't be more delighted for them. And if you made me any happier, I'd probably burst." We were still in the middle of a kiss when my phone rang. I wouldn't have taken a call from anyone but Izzy.

"Beau, are you sitting down?" Izzy asked.

"No, standing at attention, actually," I answered. Bradley's kisses always had that effect on me. "What's up?"

"Brace yourself. Gerald is in love!"

"Who is this?" I asked in mock disbelief. "That's not possible. Gerald in love? Nonsense!"

"Nevertheless, It's true. He told me so himself."

"Sounds like he's been abducted by aliens and re-placed by a creature with a heart."

"Be nice, Beau," Izzy said. "We love our Gerald."

"We know he's responsible for more erections per capita than anyone else in New York City, if that's what you mean."

"No, that is not what I mean, Beau. Gerald is head over heels for maybe the first time in his life. All right, the second time—but who's counting? Look, when Gerald fell in love with *you* way back when he had no idea what to do with it. But now he does. Maybe. So, he deserves our support."

"Yes, dear. What can I do?"

"You can come to a little gathering. And bring your perfect mate. So it has to be a Sunday, right? That's better anyway."

"Yes, an alternate Sunday. Bradley's with me to-day, praise be to all the gods. So, two weeks from now, etc."

"I'll talk to Louis and Pete. I think they're going to be in town until July. We'll come up with a date. Actually, four weeks from today makes it the first Sunday in June, so that's perfect. Before all the Pride festivities start in earnest. I'll let you know."

"Thanks for taking care of this, Iz." Bradley and I resumed our kiss, and then we paused long enough to make some highly minimal plans for the rest of our Sunday, mostly of the "What should we order in for supper?" variety. And then back to bed, of course.

Louis and Pete had the longest history of any of us, and yet they hadn't shared a bed in maybe a decade. They shared a glorious apartment—with the biggest and best Manhattan kitchen I have ever known, plus a welcoming terrace for all seasons. And, more to the point, they shared their lives. But not a bed.

Louis is perhaps the most beautiful man I have ever clapped eyes on. Certainly the sweetest. His creamy brown skin and perfect "natural" musculature allowed him the possibility of a successful modeling career. His focus and drive did the rest.

Pete is more like the Jewish uncle you never had—the one with the wicked jokes and the flawless business advice. Pete is a little lumpy—and occasionally annoying—and yet whenever I'm close to him, I feel an intense need to kiss him. Just saying.

The fact that Pete—reportedly—carries one of the longest rods God ever gifted to a mere mortal only adds to his charm, as far as I'm concerned. He makes me feel safe, actually. As if a huge cock could win battles. He's done my taxes and fended off the IRS for a decade. That's good enough for me.

It was a lovely Sunday afternoon—cool but poised to surrender to summer in a couple of weeks. Izzy and Roger arrived just after Bradley and I did, and the guys greeted them warmly as well. The beverage of the day was a sparkling wine flavored with white peaches. I'm normally skeptical of gimmicky concoctions, but I politely accepted a glass of this one. And it proved to be delicious. It was Italian, as I remember, and I made a mental note to pick up a bottle for our fridge.

I hadn't seen Roger since winter when we went to the opera together—back when I was vetting him before considering an introduction to my best friend. He was even handsomer than I remembered. "You look radiant," I said quietly.

"I'm told love does that to people," he replied. "Beau, I never thought I could be this happy. Isamu fills me with joy every moment. And it would never have happened if you hadn't agreed to introduce us."

"Yes, well, I never really gave Cupid a push before. Don't make me regret it." Roger drew back with a surprised look. I quickly added, "Sorry if I sound protective, but I've loved Izzy for a long time. I just want perfection for him. That's all."

"Tall order," Roger said, getting his smile back. "I'll do my best."

"I believe you will," I said. "Try the peach wine. It's delicious." I was suddenly aware of Bradley looking at me from across the room. He wasn't exactly glaring at me. Bradley doesn't possess a glare. But there was something in his gaze that made me wonder if I had maybe just behaved badly. Young love needs all the support it can get, after all. I should be the first to remember that. I vowed to be all-in with Roger and Izzy and never to threaten anyone again.

Gerald's arrival took my mind off the sour taste that had just developed in my mouth. Gerald was his usual glorious self with perhaps a little extra sparkle in his dangerously seductive eyes. Did the hint of silver in his temples have a new glow? Maybe. The sudden squirm in my crotch was nothing new, of course. But did Gerald greet me with unaccustomed warmth? Definitely. "Beau, please meet Asher."

I turned to see a handsome young man, about my height, with about my coloring. In fact, I imagined that he looked more like me—albeit earlier in my life—than any manchild I had ever encountered. I extended my hand to shake his, but then I drew him into an embrace as well. It seemed only fitting to welcome him into the circle. And he smelled nice.

Asher had a great smile. I liked him instantly. I also felt … pangs, I suppose. Was I jealous of Asher? Of course not. I had everything I had ever wanted with Bradley beside me and Bradley sharing my bed every night. Still…. I remembered how it felt to make love to Gerald. I remembered the ecstasy, and I remembered the deflation from the cold shoulder that always seemed to follow.

One look at Gerald told me that he had outgrown his aversion to true intimacy. So, Asher was the man to domesticate our favorite feral tomcat. Perhaps I could allow myself just a twinge of jealousy without feeling disloyal to my perfect mate. I would talk to Bradley about it. That night, after we got home. I knew he would understand.

Shortly after Gerald and Asher arrived—while I was still appraising the physical and spiritual possibilities they presented—Pete asked us all for our attention. He looked a little flushed. He also looked very sweet. And sexier than usual, I guess I'd say. "We don't get that many chances to have our best friends gathered under our roof, so here goes: Some of you met Louis's sister Louisa and her husband." Indeed I had met them. And just when I thought it impossible to be more beautiful than Louis is, they each gave him a run for the crown.

"Well, they were both killed in a car crash last week." We mostly gasped, pretty much in unison. "Yes, well, we're still processing it. But we don't have the luxury of extra time for grief because of Louis's nephew, Jared. He's staying with Louis's mother right now, but she has health issues, and she can't really make a home for him. So, he's coming to live with us. We wanted all of you to be the first to know, so we haven't told anyone else. Yet. Not even the landlord. We told Gerald, of course. We had to have his advice on how to go about the adoption."

There was a great outpouring of sympathy and support, of course. Lots of hugs. It was one of those occasions best shared with loved ones all around. "Jared must be, what, eight or nine by now?" I asked Louis.

"He'll be ten in September," Louis said. "The idea of parenting scares the shit out of me. Both of us, really. But we don't see that we have a choice. Pete has been great about this."

"Of course he has," I said. "Pete is such a mensch. You'll be so good at it! Parenting, I mean. Both of you! And you know we'll do everything we can to help." Louis held me for a while as his tears flowed down my neck. And in that moment, I truly understood the responsibility they were shouldering. And I resolved to honor my offer of help.

When Louis went into the kitchen to organize some food, I said to Pete, "This is a two-bedroom apartment."

"I noticed that," Pete said dryly.

"So, how are you going to manage this?" I asked.

"Simple. Louis is moving back into the big bedroom with me." Probably in response to my reaction, he added, "It's not such a shock, Belle. We've talked about it before. We just never had a compelling reason to rearrange our lives. Now we do. Louis's room will be perfect for Jared."

"Yes," I said, feeling quite foolish for imagining that the guys hadn't thought everything through.

"Jared can come to the studio after school and hang out in the office," Bradley said. "He can do his homework or take a nap on the sofa, or whatever he wants. Nina loves kids. She has a couple of nephews who stop by. We'll look after Jared every afternoon, if you want."

"And I volunteer weekends," I said, "except for alternate Sunday mornings. They belong to Bradley."

Izzy said, "Jared is going to have more guncles than any other kid in New York. In the world, probably." With Bradley's help, Louis laid out a buffet on the dining table. The little eggplant roll-ups were particularly tempting. Roger helped to refill glasses. It felt like a perfect, lazy Sunday afternoon in the city. I think everyone felt the circle—the ring of safety—as it eased around us.

And then Gerald said, "Since we're all together, I have an announcement to make: Asher has agreed to make me the happiest of men. We're going to be married. In July. At Fire Island Pines. And, of course, we want all of you with us." There was a brief stunned silence, followed by great whoops of joy.

When the glasses had been refilled and toasts had been proposed and the general merriment had subsided a bit, Gerald said to me, "Beau, will you give me away?"

"Of course," I said automatically, without pausing to think, *First Izzy, now Gerald! I seem to be giving away the men I love.* It was nonsensical, of course. I had everything I had ever really wanted in Bradley. And yet....

I looked around the room and saw all the people on Earth I love, plus a few people who love them. And I went right to Bradley, embraced him, and said,

Bruce K Beck

"I doubt anyone in this room is half as happy as you make me every day."

"Me too, Daddy," he said. "Me too!"

90

Tale Number Seven

Jeremy did phone me the next week. As I requested. I knew he would. That was never in doubt. I just had no idea how I would handle the situation. Did I still love him completely? Yes. Was I ready to invite him home? Not so much.

I didn't want to be a punishing partner. I wasn't even angry—perhaps—that a part of Jeremy's heart had strayed. I knew he adored me—and had, ever since I was a teen and he was a twentysomething. It was never a question of love. Until it was.

If a certain young intern in the History Department at NYU hadn't arrived on the scene, perhaps we would never have reached this impasse, Jeremy and I. And if the young intern hadn't been so bright and promising and susceptible to Jeremy's considerable charms, who knows? But if the young intern had been a handsome young man instead of a handsome young woman, I feel certain I would have kept a better grasp on the situation.

As it happened, I was off-balance for months after learning that not only was Jeremy's heart "involved" elsewhere, but that the object of his new interest was charming and pretty and very much the sort of new friend I would be pleased to make under other circumstances.

Bruce K Beck

If Morgan hadn't asked me to take Jeremy back, would I have considered it? Probably. But when she told me she was certain that Jeremy and I belong together, and that she was leaving for a new career opportunity in California, I knew I could no longer let the situation languish in the Never-never Land of What Should Be and What Might Have Been.

And yet, I neither invited Jeremy to come home nor told him to stay away. "Wally, I miss you so much I can hardly stand it," he said. As the words flowed from the speaker on my phone, I was exceptionally grateful that we were on a mere audio call—not because I hadn't even brushed my hair or made myself otherwise video-ready, but because I would have melted into a compliant mess if I had seen his handsome face at that particular moment.

"Jeremy, I need time," I said. It sounded lame even to me, but it was the truth, after all. And we left it at that. Jeremy would never have pressured me. I knew I was in charge of the timetable. I just would have preferred to be in some faraway time zone that didn't require decisions of the heart.

I talked to Ryan about it, of course. He had been my best friend and co-worker for nearly a decade, after all. We went to lunch together on a Wednesday afternoon that had both spring in the air and a stubborn dose of winter clinging to its coattails.

I told Ryan that I had not yet made a decision. About Jeremy. "What's holding you back, *mere sundar*? Perhaps I really did feel beautiful when I was with Ryan. Perhaps. With other men? Not so much.

I have a mirror. I know I'm easy enough on the eyes. But so what?

"Wally, you can't just ignore the situation," Ryan said. "I care about your happiness more than anything, and your heart will never be free to soar if you don't give Jeremy an answer. If you want him back, then tell him so. And if you don't want him back, then tell him that. He's a big boy. He knows he fucked up. He'll take his medicine."

I reached for Ryan, right there at the little table in the Greek restaurant where we had shared meals and confidences and heartaches for a decade. As I drank in his scent, I could feel Ryan's tightly muscled torso beneath his hot-pink cashmere sweater. Did that assault on my senses go right to my crotch? Of course!

"Ryan, you take my breath away," I said. "I broke up with you, and you still wanted to be my friend. I rediscovered the love of my life, and you still wanted to be my friend. I threw the bum out, and you still wanted to be my friend. And now I'm on the edge of inviting him back home, and you still want to be my friend."

"Hush, Wally," he said. "You know how simple this is. I love you. Always have. Always will. I've always thought we should live together. I'm ready to make that happen tomorrow, if it's what you want. But it has to be right for you." I gazed into my friend's beautiful eyes—the same color as the carved Tiger Eye heart pendant I gave him for Christmas—and I wondered what I had ever done to deserve him in my life. Amazing grace, indeed.

"But why me?" I asked. "You are the most beautiful man I've ever seen, Ryan. And your heart is even more beautiful than your face. Half the men in

New York would be happy to worship at your feet. Okay, maybe it's only half the *gay* men in New York. But I suspect the numbers are higher than that. Why me?"

"Because I have an unshakable belief that we belong together. You complete my soul, Wally. I've known that for a long time."

"Ryan, you know I love you," I said. "That was never the question for me."

"I know that," he said.

"Are you telling me that love isn't enough?"

"I'm telling you that love is the bedrock. Without it, we wouldn't be having this conversation. But no, it's not enough, Wally. It's enough for our friendship, true. If that's all you can give me, then I'll take it and cherish it. But what I really crave is the same devotion I feel for you."

Had there been any wind in my sails, they would have gone suddenly slack. Even the rumblings in my groin that always accompanied time spent with Ryan went silent. He had challenged my very notion of partnership, I guess. Wasn't it supposed to be about two independent creatures who come together for mutual comfort and benefit? Lots of rainbows and roses, of course, but still, two ... independent ... creatures?

Had I been missing out, all my life, on some higher plane of existence? I wasn't exactly a late bloomer or new to love, after all. I had discovered it—deep in my heart—when I was not quite fifteen. And I had never doubted the depth or the rightness of my love for Jeremy. But suddenly I didn't know quite what to do with any of it.

"Okay," I said. "You're right, Ryan. You're always right. Is that a Hindu quality?"

"No more than treachery is native to you Anglos," he said with a mischievous smile.

"That's not fair," I joked. "I'm probably more Czech than anything else."

"I believe that. Czech boys are among the prettiest in the world. But they're not famous for being stupid, Wally, while you are giving an excellent imitation of stupid right now."

"I suppose I am," I said. "I'll try to smarten up."

Did I smarten up? You will have to decide, Dear Reader. I rather floated through the next week. There were work obligations and a few minor pleasures, like celebrating the arrival of a healthy new baby born to one of our colleagues. Minor for us, of course, while major for Sarah and her husband.

It did make me wonder if I wanted a child. There was something about watching Ryan holding the tiny infant—at the office party—that gripped my insides in a primal way. Ryan was such a natural! And, of course, the baby sensed it. Newly minted little Christian settled instantly into the crook of Ryan's arm and prepared to suckle.

I knew, of course, that *I* could trust Ryan just as completely. If I so chose. And yet? There had been a time when I would have wanted nothing more than to bear Jeremy's child. With all the things that my body *can* accomplish—with strength and grace—I had indulged fantasies about things my body could *not* accomplish. And, of course, that had nothing to do with parenting or responsibility.

What is it—that desperate need to join and pro-create? Nothing to do with sex, I think. All to do with connection. I've never considered being a sperm donor, but I doubt I could get it up—not for some bank with a steady supply of liquid nitrogen, any-way.   Call me old-fashioned, but I need the connection. I need to share my outside and my in-sides with the man I adore. And, in turn, I want everything he has to offer me.

Was that the key? Could I even rely on Jeremy to give me everything he has to offer? If we had a child together, for instance, wouldn't our hearts just grow larger? That felt natural. But if another Morgan came along—or a Marvin—wouldn't I feel that I no longer had all of Jeremy? Never mind the best of him. I might retain the best. Morgan was certain I retained the best of Jeremy's heart while he was with her. But would that be enough?

I'll admit to some sleepless nights. More than I cared to acknowledge at the time. I'll admit to crying myself to sleep a few times after resisting the urge to phone Ryan and beg him to come over and hold me. It seemed so unfair. "You love Ryan," I told myself. "Yes, but you're fucking with him," another part of my heart replied.

The *noble* part of my heart won out most of the time. But there was a point in early April when the angels of my better nature surrendered. It was a Thursday. I remember it well. I asked Ryan if he would spend the weekend with me, and there was much fluttering of celestial wings as my angels abandoned me to my own devices.

"Of course, Wally," he said. "Why do you look so troubled?"

"Because I feel like an asshole."

"Because?"

"Because I keep expecting you to take care of me?" I asked. "Because I don't know if I have it in me to be the kind of friend you've been to me? Because I can't seem to make sense of the most important parts of my life? Take your pick."

"My, my!" Ryan said. "Mama used to call that *karee mein laharen*. Or something like that. I never really learned Hindi. It's probably more like 'tempest in a teapot' than anything else. Mama sends love, by the way. She adores you, you know. I think she likes you better than she likes me. But I never found that surprising."

"Ryan, how do you do this to me?"

"What do you mean, Wally?"

"How do you manage to touch my hand or smile at me or say something silly and suddenly fill my whole body with warmth?"

"No mystery there, Wally. No Eastern arts. You do the same for me. Always have. I'll bet you can figure it out if you really want to." Of course I really did want to figure it out. It seemed at the heart of my very existence. I had known since I was a child that I wanted a partner—that I needed a friend who could complete me, I suppose. Not that I applied such terminology to my inchoate feelings. I simply knew in the core of my being that somewhere there was a boy who needed me as much as I needed him.

.   Jeremy became that boy—dressed in the very handsome guise of a bright, gifted, caring young teacher. Jeremy came to work at our school just when I needed him most. Jeremy fell in love with me just as surely as I fell in love with him. Jeremy taught me that the future is possible.

When he disappeared the following school year, I was not really surprised. I may go stupid—now and then, as Ryan suggests—but I knew clearly, even at the time, that our friendship was dangerous. For both of us, probably, but especially for him. I could never have hoped to meet him again.

And yet I did. MacDougal Street will always be magical for me as a result. And so how could I not have resumed our relationship exactly where it had ended when I was still a child, really? How could I not have grabbed the man who taught me that I wanted to live and then pressed him to my heart? How, indeed?

I had loved all the getting-to-know-you, when Jeremy moved in with me. Who'd have thought his mother's name was Gladys? Who'd have thought anyone would have the slightest interest in my first dog, Bootsie? We did, it turned out. Jeremy and I. We wanted to know everything.

I would never have guessed how perfect Jeremy's ass is, or how much I would come to love the mole on his right thigh. It became like a beacon to me—a reminder that I was approaching the sweetest part of home. And when I worshiped at the altar of his manhood, I felt that I had found my destiny. My place in the world. My past, my present, and my future. My everything.

Well, that was then. It seemed an eternity ago, and yet Jeremy and I had only lived together for— five years? Nearly six, I guess. It felt like forever because that was what it was supposed to be. Until whatever happened happened. I hesitate to say, "Morgan came along," because it could have been anyone. Morgans come in many sizes, shapes, colors, and genders.

That cold, sometimes gray springtime in New York, I felt no joy when I spied my first crocus or noticed that trees were starting to bud even earlier than the year before. I took no joy in anything but the time I spent with Ryan, of course. He got me through my workday and, often, the rest of my day, too.

It took me a very long while to figure out what I was doing wrong. But then I had a sudden moment of clarity. Probably an *overdue* moment of clarity, but a moment, nevertheless. I phoned Jeremy. It was that same Thursday afternoon I had invited Ryan to share the weekend with me. I had just gotten home from work, so I figured Jeremy would probably not be in class. He answered. I had assumed he would.

"Will you spend the weekend with me?" I asked.

"Of course, Wally," he said.

"We could maybe meet at Niro's for an early supper tomorrow and then take it from there."

"Perfect."

"You don't even need to bring a change of underwear, you know," I said. "Everything you need is already here."

"I've always known that."

"Yes, well, maybe about 6:30 tomorrow?" And that's how it was arranged. But then I had to weasel out of my plans with Ryan. I felt guilty, of course. I also felt that he would understand what I was doing—probably better than I did.

"Sorry, Ry, but I hope you'll forgive me someday: I have to beg off our weekend."

"Of course, Wally," he said. "Are you okay?"

"I hope to be. The truth is, I know everything I need to know about you, Ryan, and I love you for the man you are. What I don't seem to know is Jeremy, even though I thought I'd known him for half my life. He's coming over tomorrow night and staying the weekend. I guess I'll have to do some growing up."

"I like you just the way you are," he said. "Peter Pan was always my favorite character."

"Yes, well, I'll do my best, Ryan, but I swear I feel puberty coming on. I'll make this up to you, Ry. Somehow."

"I haven't a doubt," he said. And then I felt free— or nearly free—to make sense of the weekend ahead. It had become a fact-finding mission, after all. So, what if I also craved the sweetness of Jeremy's kiss? What did it matter if half a year without Jeremy's arms around me had left me diminished? Couldn't we fix that? Couldn't we fix everything?

"Niro's pizza is not quite what it used to be," I said as I let us into the apartment on Friday night.

"No," Jeremy agreed. "But it's still better than most. The truth is, Wally, I had no interest in the food tonight. I had begun to wonder if I would ever see you again. And I've been wondering for a long time if I could survive that."

I looked into Jeremy's lovely eyes—I was never certain if they were gray or blue—and I said, "I can't handle that tonight, Jer. Let's make an appointment for talk. How about noon tomorrow? Or right after lunch? We'll talk about everything, if you want. I'll tell you anything you want to know. And I have a few questions of my own."

"Tomorrow it is."

"I'm going to have a brandy. You'll join me?"

"Of course," Jeremy said. I went to the kitchen to pour drinks, and then we settled in on the sofa to watch some Netflix, nearly as if we were picking up our lives right where they had left off. Nearly. I'll confess I snuggled in close to Jeremy just as I had always done, and when he put his arm around me—just as he had always done—it felt right as rain. Maybe. Or was it more like a monsoon?

I felt a little shaky as I was preparing for bed. Ever since September, the simple act of brushing my teeth had triggered an automatic reaction that began when I knew for certain that a portion of Jeremy's heart was elsewhere. There was something indelible about that moment just before joining him in our bed—the first time I sensed that he was no longer mine alone. It stayed stubbornly with me in the months to come. Loneliness, maybe?

But that April night, I refused to give in to thoughts of "We'll always have Paris." That April night, I was determined to make sense of my heart, my life, and my future. That April night, I slipped into bed beside Jeremy and reached for him with all the hunger that had consumed me since September. Since I was a teenager, really.

Jeremy responded with matching passion, of course. I knew he would. It was the *joy* that I had missed so desperately, I think. From the beginning, our lovemaking had been so free. So easy and natural. Whenever Jeremy and I were together, we were in each other's arms. And whether we had an hour for serious exploration or we only had time for a quick blow job, I had always felt that Jeremy worshiped me. Because he did!

I started shouting when Jeremy entered my body. It wasn't like me, and yet I had felt empty for so long. And suddenly, Jeremy was filling me again. Jeremy, my perfect fit, was around me and inside me and everywhere. Jeremy was holding my buttocks, yes, but he was also holding my heart in his hands. And my blood flowed into his. We blended. It was messy, but it was worth every moment.

When all the fluids had been shared, and all the shouts shouted, and all the sighs sighed, I lay quietly in our bed (*our* bed? I hadn't called it that for months) feeling deliciously spent. Jeremy had given me the very best of him, and I respected his gift. And yet?

Had something changed? And, if so, what? I wasn't certain about much of anything as I slipped into what I hoped would be my first proper night's sleep since Jeremy moved out—temporarily, was it? A trial separation? Is that what we were doing? And now, with Jeremy in my arms again, had he returned? I had no idea.

At breakfast, I said to Jeremy, "I know you love me, Jer, but why? I know I asked for no talk until after lunch, but I need to ask you that now."

The question had come out of left field, after all. Whatever that means. Jeremy looked a bit puzzled. He gave it his best: "Is there an answer to that question, Darling?"

"I believe there is," I said.

"I fell in love with you, Wally, the first time I saw you. You were helping to build a very silly homecoming float, and I saw you, and I thought you were the most beautiful creature on Earth. And then when you came to my office to ask for my help, I knew that my first impression was entirely accurate."

"That's the what and the when," I said. "How about why?"

"Why do *you* love *me*, Wally?"

"That's easy," I said. "Because you saved my life." That was the truth, of course. What had started as a crush on my history teacher had grown into a ... lifeline, I suppose. I was surprised that Jeremy didn't have that kind of deep connection to share. Surprised—and disappointed.

We finished breakfast, and then I said to him, "I'm sorry, Jer, but I have to ask you to go."

"But, what did I do wrong? Now, I mean?" he asked. The hurt I saw in his eyes gave me a sudden twinge of nausea. Cruelty was not my style. I hoped. But I didn't feel that I had a choice.

"It's not about right or wrong," I said. And I meant it. "It's just that I need to feel—indispensable, I guess. I don't seem to be the one for you, Jeremy. I hope you find that in your next partner. Thanks for thinking it could be me."

Jeremy didn't bother to sputter. We were past posturing. There was neither time nor space in my apartment that quiet April Saturday morning for anything extraneous. Anything dramatic. Anything beyond the simple truth.

Jeremy and I exchanged a few pleasantries and promises to keep in touch. We had history, after all. Lots of it. We shared a very deep kiss, and then Jeremy was gone. I was only paralyzed for a few minutes before I headed to the kitchen to take care of the breakfast things.

I refused to shower that Saturday morning. Or the next morning, either. There would be a time to get ready for work and the real world. Soon. Monday. Meanwhile, I knew that I would never again wear Jeremy's sweet scent on my body as an extension of who I had believed myself to be. Had he marked me? As his property? No, it was never like that. It was more that I wanted to *be* Jeremy. And when I could smell his body on mine, I felt whole. Or something. And I knew I would miss it when it was no longer mine.

I didn't call Ryan to tell him I had sent Jeremy away. I decided I needed to have my period of mourning alone. The pain was mine, after all. Whether or not I had earned it—in whole or in part—I needed to own it. I needed to sit with it and feel it until I could let it go. It didn't seem fair to drag Ryan into my mess. Besides, I would see him at the office. We might even have lunch on Monday. There would be time to make it up to him, surely. Time to deal with my mistakes, I mean. Maybe a lifetime?

This is a first edition from
Audacity Books
Please visit us on the web at
www.audacitybooks.com
For information, please send your request to
info@audacitybooks.com.

This collection of short stories is the latest offering from Bruce K Beck and Audacity Books. It completes the **Four Seasons Series—*SUMMER TALES, AUTUMN TALES, WINTER TALES,*** and now ***SPRING TALES***. Look for the **Holiday Novella Series**, which includes ***GIVING THANKS, INDEPENDENCE DAZE, MY EASTER MIRACLE,*** and ***A BUCKSKIN CHRISTMAS***. They follow Bruce's **Tolerance Trilogy—*SUCH A GOOD MAN, IT'S THEIR WAY,*** and ***THIS IS GOD'S COUNTRY***. Look for the **Obsession Trilogy—*INK OBSESSED, OPERA OBSESSED,*** and ***LOVE OBSESSED***. And the **Love Trilogy: *YOU'RE SURE TO FALL IN LOVE, LOVE AND THE EPIDEMIC***, plus ***AND LOVE ENDURES***. For updates, and for occasional gifts and offers, please subscribe at:
www.audacitybooks.com/#subscribe

Many thanks to Walter Maas for his generous wisdom, and to Richard Kutner for his classy edits. Tim Barber of Dissect Designs (www.dissectdesigns.com) signed on as a cover designer for my first novel and then became a friend. You're Sure to Fall in Love, indeed. This journey would not have been possible without the example and the teaching of Joanna Penn at www.thecreativepenn.com. I am delighted, Jo, to add this volume to your long list of books you have enabled. I'm betting you have hit your one million mark by now!

Bruce K Beck is both a writer and an accomplished chef. His novels—including the **Love Trilogy,** the **Obsession Trilogy,** and the **Tolerance Trilogy,** plus the **Holiday Novella Series**—are available online and wherever books are sold. And Bruce's **Four Seasons Series** of short stories is now complete. Before turning to fiction, Beck authored ***PRODUCE: A FRUIT AND VEGETABLE LOVERS' GUIDE***, which was called "gorgeous" by *The New York Times*, "a dazzler" by ***Bon Appetit***, and "the most spectacular food book of the year" by ***The Boston Globe***. His next book was ***THE OFFICIAL FULTON FISH MARKET COOKBOOK***, which was called "invaluable" by Jacques Pépin, and "a treasure" by Irene Sax of ***Newsday***. And Rex Reed said, "... you'll love this book. It's like a movie!"